THE CARTEL

by

Jonas Saul

PUBLISHED BY:
Imagine Press Inc.
Ebook ISBN: 978-1-927404-42-3
Paperback ISBN: 978-1-998047-10-9
Hardcover ISBN: 978-1-998047-38-3

The Cartel

The Decoy (Thirty-Three)
The Disappearance (Thirty-Four)
The Whole Truth (Thirty-Five)
Alex (Thirty-Six)
Parkman (Thirty-Seven)
Darwin (Thirty-Eight)
Aaron (Thirty-Nine)
Remains To Be Seen (Forty)

The Jake Wood Novels

The Immortal Gene (Book One)
The Immortal Target (Book Two)

Standalone Novels

'Til Death Do Us Part
The Drowning
The Woman in the Woods
The Threat
The Specter
The Mafia Trilogy
A Murder in Time
Frequency of the Dead

Co-Authored Novels

Collision Course (Written with Gary Ponzo)
There Will Be Blood (Written with Rania Stone)
The Soulless (Written with Rania Stone)

Short Story Collections

Twisted Fate (Tales of Horror)

The Cartel

Twists of Fate (Tales of Hope)

Chapter 1

Sarah Roberts entered the Mexican church under cover of night, her guns safely hidden in a bush a few feet from the large wooden doors at the front of the church. She winced as the clunk of the heavy doors resounded softly throughout the building's interior, announcing her arrival.

With one quick glance over her shoulder to ensure she wasn't being followed, Sarah slipped inside the huge Roman Catholic church on the outskirts of Tijuana.

She moved to the right, stayed close to the wall, and watched for a priest or nun to come out and greet her.

Absolute silence filled the cavernous building of worship. Pews placed in an orderly fashion started at the back and stopped near the front at a round baptismal font. She recalled one of those fonts saving her life as a church in Los Angeles exploded around her a lifetime ago.

On the opposite side of the church, scaffolding rose to

the ceiling. They were restoring sections of the interior wall. A balcony parapet thrust out of the left side of the scaffolding, its edge chipped, and the frontal area discolored with age.

With her back against the wall, she thought about her sister's note. Vivian had picked the church and the time. But to what end? To meet someone? To hurt someone? To learn where the cartel that had kidnapped Aaron, her boyfriend, was keeping him? So far, in the five days Sarah had been in Tijuana, none of the authorities had lifted a finger to go after the Enzo Cartel holding Aaron. Stagnant, languid in a hotel room, almost a week had passed while Aaron suffered somewhere close by.

Then Vivian suggested an idea. Hit the cartel man by man, piece by piece. Whittle them down. Weaken them. Then go for Aaron. Sarah had agreed. The first task was this church. Then she was off to the Baja Café a few blocks away.

Okay, Vivian, I'm in. Now what?

When no answer came, Sarah moved toward the front. Her running shoes squeaked on the wax floor. A wooden door beckoned up ahead.

In here, Vivian?

When she left the hotel at this late hour, security was changing. DEA and FBI agents were jointly managing the operation along with the Mexican authorities, but according to Vivian, that was what would get Aaron killed. The American authorities had a purpose. But they thought like Americans. They approached law enforcement like Americans do, and that worked on American soil, but down here, in Mexico, it was about who you knew or feared. With friends or associates, you could get things done. But with fear, you could accomplish anything or become paralyzed by it. Since Sarah didn't know anyone in Mexico and had no time to make acquaintances, she had to rely on fear. If she created enough fear in the Enzo Cartel, Aaron's chances of survival rose.

But how does one create fear in an organization that had mastered its livelihood on it?

Vivian said she knew how to scare the cartel and offered up her plan. It was risky and dangerous, but a plan, nonetheless. If it meant Aaron's odds of surviving rose, Sarah was in.

She reached the wooden door on the other side of the church and tried the handle. Locked.

Dammit! Why am I here, Vivian? Why bring the guns just to leave them outside? Why this church?

The internal lights had been dimmed for the night. Emergency lighting near the exits offered enough light to navigate.

She waited a heartbeat, then started across the center of the church, meandering through the pews. She crossed the middle aisle, then down between another set of pews until she reached another wooden door wedged into the side of the scaffolding.

Someone cried out, barely audible.

Sarah jolted to a stop. She didn't have to wait long to hear it again. A female cried from behind the door in front of her.

She looked around for a weapon and grabbed a steel pipe off the first level of the scaffolding.

She twisted the doorknob slowly with the pipe gripped tight in her right hand. The door opened without a sound. The room behind it was small and appeared to be an office of some kind. An old wooden desk that had seen better days sat in the corner, the top of the desk scattered with papers. Another door stood open at the back of the room. Sarah stepped inside and headed for the door at the back, her stomach doing flips.

With each step across the stone floor toward the back of the room, the female voice cried out. Sarah jerked at the harsh, distinctive sound of someone being smacked.

"Shut up, you bitch," a man's muffled voice resonated from behind the door in front of her.

The realization of what was happening in the other room came to Sarah in a rush. Anger rose in her, tightening her shoulders and neck muscles. Fueled by a sense of duty combined with fury, Sarah strode to the door, yanked it open, and brought the pipe up to strike.

What the two men were doing to the nun made her want to kill both of them. But maybe it was good that her guns were stashed in the bushes at the front of the church. She didn't want to commit murder in the House of God.

The nun was bent over a table. One man, back to Sarah, held the nun by the wrists while the other man stood behind her, his pants and underwear around his ankles. The nun's habit was cast aside in a pile on the floor. She cried silently, her eyes averted in shame, a black cloth covering her mouth to quell her screams.

Sarah had impeccable timing. The man behind the nun, his genitals exposed, was about to violate her physically.

Their eyes met.

"Señorita?" the man facing her said. "American?"

You could've prepared me better, Vivian.

"I think you came to the wrong party," he said, moving away from the distraught woman and reaching for his pants.

The man holding the nun's wrists swung his head to glare at Sarah. He let go of the nun and pivoted.

Sarah lurched forward and aimed the steel pipe at the man's collarbone. Her aim was true. The collar bone snapped like a twig underfoot in the forest, the sound corresponding with the man's scream. He dropped to the stone floor and rolled to his uninjured side, screaming and squirming.

Sarah eyed the other man, who had stopped raising his pants.

"This *is* a case of wrong place, wrong time," she shouted.

"Too bad," the man replied, his penis losing its rigidity, "you showed up. You're right, though, wrong place, wrong time for you."

"Not for me," Sarah shouted over the man wailing on the floor, waving her finger back and forth. "You are in the wrong place."

The nun slipped off the side of the table and crawled away to huddle in the corner, covering herself as best she could with her hands.

"We're *Halcones* for the Enzo Cartel. The eyes and ears."

Ahh, okay, Vivian. I see your angle better now.

The man moved closer, not caring that he was half-naked. "We're like spiders. Once in our web, you never get out." He licked his lips and roved Sarah's body with his eyes, starting at her feet and stopping at her breasts. "You'll do fine. Hey Miguel, we got us a hot nun for fun. But this one, she'll just add to the party."

Sarah moved a step back to prepare for her lunge. That simple movement saved her life as the man on the floor suddenly turned, raised his good arm with a gun, and fired wildly at Sarah.

Without thinking, acting purely on instinct, Sarah pitched forward, shoved the pipe into the man's shoulder, and grabbed for the gun.

The man, weakened by the pain in his broken collar bone, the pipe now jamming into him, weakened his grip. Sarah deftly yanked the gun from his grasp and spun it around to aim at him as he squirmed.

Then she fired.

A hole opened in the would-be rapist's chest. His eyes widened, and his scream echoed throughout the small room.

Sarah brought it up to bear on the other man before he moved two steps closer.

"Oh, little girl." The man stood five feet away, his mouth in a condescending smirk. "You're dead. You have no idea what you just did." His Spanish accent worsened as his anger increased. "You're so dead. In the worst possible way."

Blood bubbled from the man's chest on the floor as he gagged.

Shit, Vivian, Casper's going to be pissed about this.

The last man standing raised his hands waist high.

"Señorita, put the gun down."

The nun had quieted in the corner. She had taken her black habit and covered her body with it like a blanket.

Sarah shrugged one shoulder. "Wrong place, wrong time, eh? You shouldn't have been here. What Cartel did you say you were with?"

"The Enzo Cartel. But maybe we can let this go if you just put the gun down. Walk out of here, and we'll see if we can forget this ever happened."

The guy writhing on the ground moaned through gritted teeth as his shirt soaked through with blood. "Fuck that," he managed to say. "She dies for this. But a hundred men rape her first."

"Now, now," his partner said. "No one's raping no one today. Ain't that right, Señorita?"

"Kick off your pants," Sarah said.

"What?"

"You want to live? Kick off your pants. Then shove them over to me."

He didn't move.

Sarah rushed up and whacked him in the jaw with the pipe. She swung around him and set the gun against the man's ear while he moaned.

"I don't fucking care what cartel you work for. Remember my name. Sarah Roberts. Memorize it. Take it back to your boss, your drug lord, the *Capos*. I have a message to deliver. Now, kick off your pants, or I will kill you."

He hesitated another few seconds, then used his feet to pull out of them. The nun remained quiet under cover of her habit.

"Tell whoever matters in the Enzo Cartel that they came after the wrong person." Sarah thought of Aaron, his captivity, his missing finger. Then Vivian invaded her consciousness and whispered what she needed to do.

Sarah glanced at the nun holding the habit up to her neck. She was young, no more than her mid-twenties. Had she been raped, Sarah wondered how she could ever come back from that as a nun. Hopefully, what happened wouldn't stop the nun from remaining in her faith.

"Take off your shirt," Sarah told the man still standing.

"You can't be serious," he mumbled.

His jaw was swelling fast, but it didn't appear to be dislocated. Sarah raised the pipe in a warning.

"Okay, okay."

He pulled the shirt over his head and dropped it to the floor. Now he was completely naked.

Sarah lowered the gun and shot a bullet into the naked man's right foot just below the ankle.

He dropped to the floor beside his friend, his hands wrapping the wound as if that would take the pain away. Sarah kicked his underwear out the open door and grabbed his dirty pants. She walked over to the nun and set the pants down, keeping an eye on the men in case they had another gun concealed somewhere.

"Take these." Sarah pushed the pants closer. "Cover yourself until you can get another habit."

"But Señorita," the nun said through her tears, her voice surprisingly strong for what she had just endured. "I have this one."

Sarah shook her head. "I need this one. That's why I came here tonight."

The nun looked at the habit, then the jeans, and back to the habit.

"Take it," she said.

Sarah slipped the habit over her head as the nun put the jeans on. Her breasts were covered in a too-tight sports bra, but Sarah figured she had enough clothes on now to get to wherever she slept in the church.

The man with the bubbling chest wound had grown quiet. His eyes were glazed over, and his breathing shallow.

The other man held his bleeding foot and cried like a baby, breathing through clenched teeth.

"You're gonna pay for this," he stammered.

"Just remember my name." She came around until she was facing him, the habit a bit big for her, flowing out like a dress. "Sarah Roberts. And I'm here to kill the Enzo Cartel. Send the message. No one lives. Got it? No one lives."

Sarah adjusted the cowl of the habit until only her face showed through. The veil protruded outward, covering her face from side view. Now that the nun was standing, Sarah saw they were physically about the same size.

"You ever heard of stigmata?" Sarah asked the Mexican holding his foot.

"What?" he shouted, his voice cracking, his mouth barely opening.

The other Mexican had stopped breathing. His dead eyes stared at the ceiling.

"What's my name?" Sarah asked.

The man repeated it perfectly.

"Good."

As the nun exited through the door, Sarah kicked the man on the stone floor. She hated rapists. They weren't worth the bullet that killed them.

She understood why Vivian brought her here. It was as much for the nun's habit as it was to stop the violation. The hatred for what rapists did, the stealing of innocence, was something Sarah never needed to see again, but she also understood that she would never escape. It was her life now, her job. Sarah was in a unique position with Vivian to be able to hurt these kinds of people. As much as she never wanted to be near them again, there was no way she could avoid it.

Because of that, she was the one who got to choose their penalty.

With the gun on an angle, she jammed it onto the back of the man's right hand and pulled the trigger.

Over his screams, she tried to explain that he now had two signs of the stigmata. Hopefully, he would find religion after this and leave the Enzo Cartel.

"Because if you don't leave the cartel on your feet, you'll leave on your back, in a casket or a mass grave like some of your victims." She turned around at the door. "You were at the wrong place, wrong time. Soon my name will strike fear in the Enzo Cartel. Tell them I'm here. Send the message. Sarah Roberts says no one lives."

She left the room as the lone Mexican bellowed a horrific tune of pain. Outside, she dumped the Mexican's gun and grabbed her own. Once her weapons were securely fastened to her body under the habit, she picked up her one knife. Knives were silent. Guns were loud. Sometimes a kill needed to be quiet.

Then she started down the road to the café she was supposed to visit tonight. A couple of deep breaths loosened the tightness in her shoulders.

Vivian said she would locate a lieutenant of the Enzo Cartel at the café. This *lugarteniente* held the second highest position in the cartel, and, according to Vivian, he was having a drink with some of his men—*Halcones*—at the Baja Café three blocks from the church. He would recognize Sarah, but perhaps not in a nun's habit.

The darkened Mexican street didn't give her black figure away as she moved toward the café like a ghost in the night, keeping to the shadows.

It was only a matter of time before the cartel released Aaron to turn off the pressure she was about to mount. Vivian claimed there was no other way. Raids and arrests by the DEA and the Mexican *federales* would only cause Aaron's death.

Sarah had to do this her way, as she always did.

They'd release Aaron soon.

Or she would kill them all.

No one lives.

She banished thoughts of Aaron as the café came up on her right.

Chapter 2

Casper pulled the curtain aside and peered into the hotel's parking lot. Overwhelmed with frustration, he'd found sleep elusive the last few nights. Sarah was driving him mad with her constant badgering. One week in Mexico, and nothing had happened. Red tape. Multi-agency bullshit.

His hands were tied. So far, there had been nothing he could do about it. As in Amsterdam, if the local authorities didn't offer carte blanche, he had to wait and do things their way.

This was Mexico, not America. The kidnapping of a Canadian man didn't raise the American or Mexican stakes too high.

Mexico's DFS, *Dirección Federal de Seguridad*, or Federal Security Directorate, and the Municipal Judicial Federal Police, also known as *Federales*, were assigned to aid in the DEA's every need. Buck Schaffer, known as Casper to his colleagues, had arrived in Tijuana with Sarah as an adviser to the DEA. The joint task force was supposed to enter the Enzo Cartel compound strategically and shut them down, in addition, to finding and releasing the Canadian, Aaron Stevens, but the bickering about how that was supposed to happen had gone on too long.

Aaron didn't have the luxury of waiting.

Casper had no idea what he would tell Sarah in the morning, as another day would probably pass without action.

Each team argued who would lead the strike on the cartel, with neither one agreeing that the Americans could have point on it. Since they wouldn't allow the Americans to lead the raid, it had to be the DFS or the *Federales*. But neither felt the Enzo Cartel was big enough to bother with, especially for one man.

It was brought up in a PowerPoint presentation—a *fucking* PowerPoint presentation—that collapsing the Enzo Cartel at this early date was like spraying a wasp nest during the daylight while the wasps weren't there. All you did was kill the hive. The wasps would build another.

The DFS wanted to wait until the Enzo Cartel was big enough to put a dent in the opium and cocaine heading over the border since they were a relatively new and small organization. The *Federales* weren't interested in attacking a cartel to save one Canadian man. Thousands of Mexicans were kidnapped yearly. Tens of thousands were murdered annually. Why was this one man so important? Because his girlfriend was here? Because she was important to the American government?

That wasn't good enough. So they waited. And they debated. And Casper kept Sarah up to date but trimmed the information some. If she knew the truth, she'd freak out on him. If she knew a raid wasn't imminent, and the likelihood dimmed with each new day, she might do something reckless.

So what was next? If not today, it would be tomorrow when Sarah would do more than demand answers. And then what would happen? Probably the Mexicans would arrest her, detain her, and one of the authorities on the *mordida*—on the take, accepting bribes—would seal her fate while she was in prison, and the Enzo Cartel would have their wish granted. Because that was the cartel's main goal. Kill Sarah Roberts for costing them millions in laundered money when she shut down a human trafficking club in Toronto.

Casper let the curtain fall back into place. He turned to face the darkened room and contemplated Sarah's psychic ability. What he saw her do in Amsterdam was incredible. He grew to respect her. She was strong, confident, and quite an admirable opponent. Bringing her to Mexico to be there when Aaron was freed had been the plan since they landed in Amsterdam.

If she had died in Europe, the cartel would've disposed of Aaron, and the DFS and the Federales would've gotten their wish to watch, wait, and monitor.

But Sarah didn't die. He had placed the right calls and got the right people set up, only to be stopped at this shitty hotel on the outskirts of Tijuana, waiting for *nothing* to happen.

Going against policy and doing it his way would piss off the Mexicans. Collaborating with Sarah and using her psychic ability, if she would, to release Aaron could prove to be exciting and dangerous. But could they do that and leave the country without repercussions? He thought not.

Casper was valuable to his superiors back home. The consequences would be light. They needed him. They signed off on this assignment. He was supposed to return to the States with Aaron free and Sarah in tow.

But any cowboy stuff would hurt relations with the Mexican authorities and potentially damage future cooperation.

Did that matter to him? How important was Sarah? If Aaron was left behind, how important would she be then?

He shook his head in the darkroom at the notion that Aaron could ever be left behind. That certainly wasn't an option. But until now, the Mexicans were sealing Aaron's fate by keeping Sarah secluded in this hotel. Soon, one of Enzo's men would hear that Sarah was in Tijuana. They would come. Sarah would be taken. She would be tortured, flayed with an onion peeler, torn apart, and killed for destroying their money laundering operation. Then Aaron would die.

And for what? So more drugs could be sold on American streets?

Casper had to put a stop to this. He had to act. But how? Without backup, any operation was suicide unless Sarah's sister offered a way in and a way out. Something only an entity with the power to see things from the other side could offer.

He snapped his fingers.

"There has to be a way," he said to the empty room.

Once dressed, he silently opened his hotel room door and checked for the security detail. A lone man sat on a chair by the elevators. He leaned on the table, a newspaper dangling over the edge, his AR-15 strapped to the back of his chair.

Casper eased his door closed. At the phone, he dialed the room-to-room feature and called Sarah's number, rocking back and forth on his heels. She would either chew him out or agree they had to do something. The waiting around was probably driving her more mad than him.

After five rings, he set the phone down. She was sleeping. Of course, she would be at this hour.

But fuck it. He needed an answer.

He dialed out again.

After ten rings, an odd premonition that something wasn't quite right swept over him. He set the phone down softly, going over ideas in his head. Why wasn't she answering? If she wasn't in her room, where could she be?

He dialed the front desk. The clerk answered on the second ring.

"Good evening, Mr. Schaffer. How can I assist you?"

"Have you seen the occupant of room 510 this evening? Sarah Roberts?"

"No sir, not since I saw you with her in the restaurant here in the lobby earlier this evening. Why? Is something wrong?"

"I just tried her room, but she didn't answer."

"Probably sleeping, sir."

Casper thought about it. Certain people slept at different degrees. Some were light sleepers. Others could slumber through a tornado.

"You're probably right."

Casper hung up and headed back to his door. He opened it, eased out of the room, and started down the hall to Sarah's room. His footfalls on the carpeted hotel floor made no noise.

The guard by the elevators didn't move.

At the door to Sarah's room, he knocked lightly.

After half a minute with no answer, he knocked harder, his stomach twisting. Could they have gotten to her? On the fifth floor?

It couldn't be. Security was tight. This operation had a combined force of nearly fifty men, with a dozen taking rotating shifts guarding the hotel's exterior.

Unless someone was accepting bribes. He had to consider that. A bribe or two later, and a small bomb could be delivered to Sarah's door. Or *sicarios*—gunmen, hitmen—could be offered a free pass.

He knocked harder. The guard by the elevator didn't budge. Casper frowned, his internal radar pinging. He needed his weapon. He needed to sound the alarm.

First, he needed inside her room.

He ran for his own room, fumbled the key card, finally got inside, and dashed across the floor for his service weapon. He chambered a round and grabbed the phone by the bedside to ring the front desk again.

"Good evening, Mr. Schaffer. How can I be of service?"

"Bring up a room key for Sarah's room, number 510."

"But sir—"

"Something's wrong," Casper shouted. "Just do it, or I'll shoot the lock off the door and break into her room."

Casper slammed the phone down and ran from the room. Once in the corridor again, he turned toward the guard.

"Hey, wake up," he shouted. "Going into room 510 to check on Sarah Roberts."

The guard didn't move.

"You listening to me?" Casper screamed as he made it to

Sarah's door. "Wake the fuck up, asshole!"

Casper closed his hand into a fist and punched Sarah's door. "Wake up, Sarah. We need to talk."

He kept his gun down by his thigh. Something had happened to the guard at the elevators. He still wasn't moving. The front desk clerk could be compromised as well. If that were the case, when the elevator doors opened, a trio of masked gunmen would exit and punch holes into his body from twenty feet away.

He spun around on his heels and ran for the exit sign. Gunmen would be coming up the stairs as well. Everything would be guarded. He was trapped.

At the exit door, he slammed into it sideways, shoved the door open, and then jumped back. Nothing happened. No one shot at him.

He stepped inside the door, leaving it open a crack to watch the corridor. After a short wait, a young Mexican male dressed in the hotel's uniform exited the elevator, glanced at the security guard, shook his head slightly, and started toward room 510, a key dangling from his palm.

The clerk was a short, rotund male in his early twenties. The buttons on his shirt, a size too small, had been undone at the collar.

Casper came out of the stairwell, his gun aimed at the clerk.

The clerk stopped short of room 510, his eyes widening.

"What?" the clerk gasped. "What's going on?"

"What's your name, kid?"

"Hernandez." It came out in a squeak.

"Okay, Hernandez, take it easy. Here's how this is going to work. Continue walking to room 510. Once there, insert the key and open the door. Then I need you to leave the door ajar and return to the front desk. If I need you again, I will call."

Hernandez shook his head up and down rapidly, sweat already forming on his round face. His breathing turned ragged. Air came and went in short, timed gasps.

"Do it now," Casper said when Hernandez hadn't moved.

Dazed, his lower lip quivering, Hernandez raised the key and aimed it for the slot in room 510's door handle. Casper remained in a shooter's stance, feet wide, arms outstretched in a firing position similar to the one he would use at the firing range.

The key card slipped inside the knob without resistance. Casper prepared to leap back if someone rigged the door to blow. But nothing happened. The door opened with ease.

"Now go back downstairs. Speak nothing of this. I will call you within five minutes."

Hernandez walked backward for a few paces, then turned and jostled down the hall toward the elevator, his trousers audibly rubbing at his inner thighs. Casper waited as Hernandez pushed the elevator button. The elevator hadn't been called to another floor, so the door opened instantly. When Hernandez disappeared inside and the door shut, Casper lowered his weapon and moved in front of Sarah's door.

He pushed it all the way open, keeping himself to the side. By the empty bed, the lamps shone to illuminate an empty room.

Sarah was gone.

Casper entered the room to find no signs of struggle. Even the bed was still made up.

"Shit!"

Where did she go? Willingly or forced?

He jumped back into the corridor and ran for the security guard by the elevator, who hadn't moved the entire time.

"Hey, wake up." He touched the guard's shoulder. "Wake up, asshole." He shook the man. When he got no response, Casper checked his pulse.

There wasn't one.

"Fuck. What the hell?"

The elevator dinged beside him. Something metallic clicked from inside the elevator. It sounded like a gun was being readied.

Casper sprinted for his open room door.

The elevator opened behind him.

He was too far from his room. He wasn't going to make it in time. Ten feet. Eight feet. A cold sheen covered him as if he had just run through the blast of an air conditioner.

Movement behind him. Footsteps entered the corridor.

He waited for the bullet.

His open door came up on the right. When no bullet came, he dove inside the room, rolled on the floor, and smacked into the base of the bed.

Scrambling on his hands and knees, he crawled behind the open door and looked through the crack to watch the hallway.

The worst thing about his job were these tense moments. Not knowing what was going on or who was involved. How could they circumvent security? Even in moments like this, he felt fear, which was rational. But fear did strange things to the human body. In Casper, it heightened all five senses. His hearing became acute, his eyes wide. It was his breathing, rapid and loud, that scared him. It could very well be the one thing that gave him away. If these were cartel men and they saw him, he was as good as dead.

Did Vivian warn Sarah to leave tonight because the Enzo Cartel was staging a hit on her? If so, why didn't she tell him about it? If the attack on the hotel couldn't be stopped, at least she could've saved his life.

Thanks, Sarah!

Sarah would have to explain herself if he made it out of this.

He forced his breathing to slow down, to get quieter, then waited behind his room's door, staring out into the hallway until his vision blurred. Then it wavered. He blinked, refocused his eyes, and wiped his moist hands on the carpet to remove the sweat building up.

A man wearing a black balaclava leaped into sight. He carried a *chanate*—Spanish for great-tailed grackle—which was an M4 carbine with a grenade launcher strapped to his chest, the barrel end waiting to do business. Casper recognized the beta C-mag double drum magazine, what was commonly called, *huevos de toro*—bull's testicles.

What the fuck?

These hitmen meant business. Cartel business.

They must've known Sarah was heavily protected. With firepower like this, how did Casper not hear any resistance?

Another man came into view. Casper raised his weapon. His little gun was like bringing a knife to a gunfight. The M4 carbine would cut him in half before he could get two shots off.

His vision blurred again. The floor wavered left, then right, slanting, then tilting. His leg stung like a bee had attacked him.

He looked down and saw a dart protruding from his calf below the knee.

What the hell?

He understood what happened as his equilibrium wavered. They shot him with a tranquilizer instead of bullets as he ran for his hotel room.

His legs weakened, and his stomach turned as dizziness settled over his system.

It had to be Special K. What else worked that fast? Unless they meant to kill him like the guard by the elevator.

Casper dropped his gun as he fumbled with the weight of it, then fell sideways from behind the door. The room's ceiling spun.

Five masked faces entered his room and stood in a semi-circle, looking down. Their faces filled up the part of the ceiling he had been trying to focus on.

"Where's Sarah Roberts?" one of the men grunted in a Spanish accent.

Casper closed his eyes, fading fast. Sarah made it. She got out. They wouldn't have asked that question if they had her. Sarah had left, not just him, but them, too.

Good luck out there, Sarah ... run, baby, run.

One of the men ordered another to take Casper to the vehicle. They would learn what he knew, one way or another.

His eyes closed.

Chapter 3

OLD CARS LITTERED THE street in front of the Baja Café. Sarah felt like she'd gone back in time. Most were from the fifties, with a few from the sixties. One vehicle stood out. A shiny new Mercedes parked near the front of the café. One man sat behind the wheel, puffing on a cigarette. Two men guarded the entrance to the café—and the Mercedes—along with at least two more men across the street.

Sarah eased farther back in the shadows, watching, waiting. It was prudent—life-saving—to know how many men guarded the front and how many were stationed at the back.

Whoever the lieutenant was, the man inside the Baja Café that she had come to meet, he was important enough to warrant his own security detail. Would this lieutenant know about Aaron and be willing to impart any of that information? The probability of learning anything willingly was remote.

She would have to convince him to tell her. But how could she accomplish that and leave the café alive?

Their agenda was to capture her. Her agenda was to remain free. There had to be a better way than what Vivian had planned. But with Casper's people—the authorities—tied up behind bureaucracy and Vivian offering this chance, Sarah had to move forward, reckless though it may be.

Covered head to toe in the nun's habit, Sarah emerged from the darkness, walked across the street, and slipped alongside the building. The stone walkway to the back was old and cracked. Litter strewn along the edges of the stones hadn't been picked up in months. Only weeds survived where they could.

At the back of the building, she stopped to listen. Other than the dull thud of music from inside the café and the crickets chirping outside, nothing moved or made a sound. Something heavy, like a truck, drove by slowly on the street out front.

Sarah lowered to her haunches, touched each weapon she carried to ensure everything was secure, and then continued to wait. She studied the darkness beyond the single light that floated above the back door of the café. After ten minutes, convinced the back wasn't guarded by anyone outside, she approached the door.

Headlights flashed along the road behind her.

She darted back to the safety of darkness to wait out the approaching vehicle.

It sounded like the same one from moments before. A heavy truck of some kind. The engine's growl eased off as it got closer, gravel crunching under its tires.

Sarah slipped her hand inside the nun's habit and gripped

her semi-automatic. If need be, she could easily lift, aim, and shoot the weapon through the habit.

The vehicle came into sight. An H2 Hummer. American made.

She remained where she was as the vehicle stopped outside the back of the café, the engine idling. It could be her people looking for her. But how would they know to come here? She'd told no one where she was going.

It could also be cartel members driving an armored vehicle. Maybe they had arrived at the back door to pick up the lieutenant. If that were the case, was this a wasted trip?

She waited. The Hummer idled.

The café's back door opened. The Hummer pulled out and drove away maddeningly slow as if on some sort of cue.

Sarah took her chance and crept toward the open back door. Voices resonated from inside the café, growing louder as she eased closer.

With her right hand holding the semi-automatic, finger inside the trigger guard, she walked around the open door and stopped in front of a huge man. The butt of a handgun protruded from his belt, and at least a twelve-inch blade was strapped to his thigh.

His dead eyes turned to her. Playing the role of a nun, Sarah edged past the man as he said something to her in Spanish.

Vivian translated in her head.

You're up late, sister.

Sarah nodded as she meandered through the grimy kitchen, past a tiny Mexican boy cleaning a burnt pot in a large sink and through two swinging doors that led into the main café area.

Tension filled the air in the room the second the swinging doors stopped. The bartender was serving two men at the far side of the bar. He placed their drinks down tentatively, his eyes on Sarah.

There had to be fifteen men in the café, which doubled as a bar at this hour. All eyes were on her. The nun's habit was perfect for hiding her identity and the weapons. But it was an attention grabber as well.

She strode along the length of the bar and found a seat near the front where her back could be at the wall. Then she pointed at the bottle of gold tequila and nodded.

With her head hung low, she waited them out. Eventually, the noise rose to a pre-Sarah din.

A moment later, the gold tequila was placed in front of her.

"Haven't seen you in here before," the bartender said. "I know all the nuns from the church."

"I'm with the Order of the Holy Christ Church," she whispered, hoping there was such a thing and hoping there weren't any religious experts among the crowd. Although from the looks of them, the likelihood of a religious expert was dim.

"English," he said. "American. Here visiting?"

He had spoken English to her without her catching on. He'd pegged her as American before they'd even said one word to one another.

Some of the others still watched them. One man stood out. He sat in the middle of the café surrounded by three men who belonged on the glossy covers of protein drink containers. All three were obviously armed, their shoulder holsters revealed behind their open jackets. That had to be the lieutenant and his muscle.

"Yes," Sarah said. "Visiting." She swished her beverage and stared down at the gold liquid, her right hand still inside her habit.

The bartender moved away. Maybe she should leave. Wait for the lieutenant outside. She'd only have to deal with his guards then. Inside, she would have to deal with over a dozen men.

Before she could drop a foot onto the dirty floor of the café, someone sidled in beside her.

"Hey, sister, how can I help?"

He was young, in his early twenties, clean-shaven, and spoke English without an accent.

"You're from around here?" she asked, carefully examining the lieutenant and his bodyguards.

"Born in California, but Mexico is my home now. What's a nun doing here at this hour?"

"Please tell me that's not a pick-up line."

He studied her with a scrutiny borne of suspicion and distrust. Could the entire café be filled with Enzo Cartel men? If so, why were they within walking distance to the hotel Casper had her holed up in for the past week? Why didn't the authorities raid this place?

After a moment, the young man glanced at the lieutenant's table, then looked away. Something changed in his face. He acted flustered, fiddled with his hands briefly, then twisted in his chair and turned to leave.

"Look, sister," he whispered. "You should leave and never come back. The men here don't care much for religion getting involved in their business."

Sarah turned, her face pensive, offering nothing. "Their

business is with God whether they like it or not. We all have business with God."

The man walked away, hit the front door, and left the café. She turned back in her chair and swished her drink again.

What next? Leave? Wait outside?

C'mon Vivian. Speak to me.

Since nothing was forthcoming, Sarah decided to leave. Outside, she would have fewer men to deal with. Outside, they would be more cautious with their weapons. Inside, the café walls shielded them. There were simply too many men to handle on her own.

This feels like a mistake, Vivian. Why am I here?

Sarah sampled the tequila. She wondered if this would be logged as one of the stupidest things she had ever done. Entering the Baja Café where over a dozen cartel members were lounging after searching for her.

This task was different, though. This one was a rescue mission. Aaron was in trouble. The men around her knew where he was being held. At least one of them had probably seen him recently. It was even possible that the man who cut Aaron's finger off was here, in this café. This was as much a personal war as when she had freed the victims of human trafficking in Toronto and Europe. And she did that with the risk of great personal harm. So why not be a little reckless in the quest to locate her Aaron?

But that wasn't all of it. Aaron's abduction was partly her fault. Stopping the Torture Club in Toronto had hurt the cartel's money laundering partner. When she shut them down in Toronto, she cost the cartel considerable time and money, and they wanted recompense.

But they didn't realize that Sarah never offered recompense, and by demanding it of her, they had forced her hand. She would stay. She would find a way to isolate the lieutenant and get the answers she needed. She would find Aaron even if all law enforcement agencies worked against her. She would do it because she had to. There was no other option. If she risked her life for strangers as much as she did, she could damn well risk her life for Aaron—ten times over.

She drank the rest of the tequila in one gulp and dropped the glass on the top of the bar harder than she wanted to.

The bartender glanced her way, then started over.

"Do you plan to be a nun for the rest of your life?" he asked.

"Short life?"

"Why are you here?"

"The tequila."

"That could be a dangerous drink."

"How dangerous?"

He turned away and refilled her glass. After placing it in front of her, he walked to the end of the bar, grabbed a stained white towel, and began wiping his glasses down.

She swished the drink, staring into it. When movement by the lieutenant's table caught her eye, she resisted the urge to look up. They might see her watching. Notice her interest. She waited, listening to their footfalls among the noise of the patrons.

Are they leaving?

She lifted her glass and drank from it, which offered a chance to see where they were headed. One of the lieutenant's apes followed him toward the restroom. The other two remained at the table.

This was her chance. Isolate him in the toilet. Hurt him, get answers, then leave. Other than the one guard following him into the restroom, no one needed to be the wiser.

"Where's the restroom?" she asked.

The bartender pointed to where the lieutenant had just gone.

Sarah nodded and eased off her chair. Without noticeably hurrying, she needed to get in there in case the lieutenant pissed fast. Walking by him on the way out wouldn't work.

With each step, her grip on the butt of the weapon hidden under the nun's habit remained firm. The likelihood of them having made her and this being an ambush was remote, but she couldn't take the chance.

Her heart beat like a starving, demented bird fighting against her ribcage. Inside her arid mouth, the tequila's aftertaste nauseated her. The confrontation about to happen weakened her resolve more than any other. In the past, this sort of thing promised consequences for others. But the consequences, in this case, would be felt by Aaron, her man, her beloved.

And that was unacceptable.

Her grip tightened until pain echoed through the joints in her hand.

These assholes had taken Aaron. They had cut him, hurt him irreparably. She had to hurt them one by one until either she felt better about it or Aaron was released. She didn't want to think about what she would do if Aaron died while still their prisoner.

The hall leading to the restrooms was filthy. A black grime or mold crawled up the walls from the baseboards. The female door advertised a woman in a skirt, and the male door had a picture of a man wearing a sombrero.

After a glance over her shoulder, she eased the knife out from under her habit. With a soft touch to avoid unnecessary noise, she pushed open the door to the men's room. If the bodyguard had leaned against it, the scuffle would warn the others, but no one waited by the door. Sarah took one more look behind her and slipped inside the men's restroom.

A wall abutment concealed her from the toilets, urinals, and sinks. Thankful the door had a thumb lock, she secured the door, then put her back to the wall. The knife comforted her as she tightened her grasp. She held it so the blade was parallel to her forearm, aiming outward. It allowed her to punch easily and slice with the blade without much effort. Her other hand remained available for either gun, still concealed under the habit.

The smell emanating from the urinals was disgusting. It was worse than an outhouse at an outdoor concert. At least that had ventilation. The scent of urine-soaked walls and feces-covered toilets offered her a chance to vacate last night's dinner without much effort.

She took two deep breaths and let them out slowly, preparing to round the corner as a toilet flushed.

A sink turned on. She took a look. The bodyguard was bent over the sink washing his hands. She eased out of hiding further. The lieutenant was nowhere in sight.

Below the guard's shiny black shoes, water had seeped out from under the filthy, water-stained wall. A small puddle had formed near a drain in the center of the floor that didn't seem to be in the lowest spot anymore. With no caution sign, anyone could slip on that water and brain themselves on the dirty tile floor.

But something told Sarah this restroom, and by extension, this café, wasn't high on the list for tourists.

When her eyes cut to the mirror, the guard stopped moving and watched her, the water still running in the sink. Slowly, he turned off the sink, wiped his hands on his pants, and turned to address her.

"You're in a dangerous position, sister," he said.

Before she could temper her tongue, Sarah replied, "I'm a bride of Christ. Nothing earthbound is dangerous. I exist here. Then I will die and exist with the Lord."

"Who are you talking to?" the lieutenant asked from one of the stalls.

The guard's eyes dropped to Sarah's hand. The subtle movement, a muscle spasm under his right eye, told her he'd seen the knife.

His hand slipped inside his jacket. "Dangerous position," he repeated.

Sarah lurched forward two steps, pumped her arms, and jumped feet first toward the water puddled on the floor as if she was stealing second base. Her right arm extended, the knife reflecting light into her eyes. Sarah slid by the guard's feet and smacked into the wall behind him. But not before gouging his right ankle and Achilles tendon with the sharp knife as she slid by.

A quick twist and she was on her knees, the knife up to defend herself.

When he turned around, he applied weight on his right side. His knee buckled, and a look of confusion creased his face.

Sarah rapidly got to a standing position, the wall to her back. The water from the floor had seeped through the habit, and the horrid smell of the toilets was even closer now.

The guard tried to stand on his foot again, but something wasn't quite right.

"What's going on?" the lieutenant asked.

"Uhm, I ahh," the guard managed to say before he saw the blood pooling under his right heel. While leaning on his left foot, he lifted his wounded one as if he was looking for gum on the bottom of his shoe.

Sarah was more interested in what he had pulled out of his jacket. When she saw the brass knuckles clamped in his right fist, she breathed a sigh of relief. Had it been a gun, she'd have to pull hers, and then weapons would be fired, and the noise would alert the rest of the café.

He set his right foot down gently and glanced at her with what looked like a cross between fear and anger. He stumbled toward her, raising his fists.

"You'll be skinned alive for that," he muttered through clenched teeth.

The pain was settling in over his system. He couldn't apply any weight to the right side now. Blood oozed out faster and faster.

"Stop, or I will kill you," Sarah whispered.

"Good luck."

"Who's out there?" the lieutenant asked.

"A dead nun," the guard responded. "Only a stupid, dead nun."

He thrust forward and drove his brass-knuckled fist at her face. She dropped under it, the guard's fist barely skimming the top of her head, and swung the knife's blade in an arc across his lower stomach where the collared shirt he wore had slipped out of the top of his pants.

He moaned, moved away, and hopped on his left foot until he was leaning against the wall.

"You bitch!" he yelled, looking down as blood soaked the top of his pants.

At least two shades of red seeped from his face as he slowly slid down the wall until he was in a sitting position. The blood from his ankle wound had intensified, and now he held his intestines with both hands.

She couldn't look away or leave him alone to deal with the lieutenant because he was still armed. As soon as she turned her back, a bullet would enter it.

"This is for Aaron."

She stepped close, pulled her right leg back far and wide, and like a quarterback, kicked a field goal using the guard's face. She hit him so hard his head bounced off the wall, denting it slightly, then slumped down and dangled, resting on his upper chest.

"What the fuck is going on?" the lieutenant shouted as he moved around frantically inside the stall.

Someone tried the bathroom door. Then they pounded on it, asking in Spanish what was going on.

"Everyone okay?" someone else shouted.

"Yes," Sarah shouted back. "Stay out."

She reached inside the guard's suit jacket, grabbed the bodybuilder's weapon, aimed at the base of the restroom door, and fired twice into the outer hallway. Someone yelled, someone grunted, and the voices moved away.

She turned her attention to the stall that still concealed the lieutenant. What was he up to? Preparing his own weapon for when she opened the door?

Fear motivated people, so she decided to scare him out.

Using the bodyguard's gun, she fired into the stall doors on either side of the lieutenant's stall. The unpainted, dirty wooden door on the left cracked where the bullet entered. The one on the right buckled inward and was almost torn from its hinges.

"Coming out?" she asked.

"Fuck you. Come and get me."

"Not appetizing. I'll pass."

"You'll be eating your own intestines when I'm done with you. I'll see to that."

"Whatever. Your threats are meaningless. Cartels are only men. Albeit crazy, insane, loco men, but still, just men. And men bleed. Men can be killed. That means the Enzo Cartel can be killed. Come out now, or you will be added to the list of cartel men I've killed tonight."

She fired the bodyguard's last two bullets above the lieutenant's stall. Pieces of the wall chipped and rained down inside the stall.

"Okay, okay, I'll come out. Stop fucking shooting."

The lock on the door cracked. Then the door eased open on noisy hinges. Sarah had to fight not to gag at the fetid smell wafting through the disgusting restroom.

The lieutenant looked at his guard and laughed a short, sharp burst. "Get a load of this shit." He stepped all the way out as someone yelled from inside the café. "Religion makes me sick." He nearly spat the words. "More people have died in the name of God than in any cartel business, and we're the ones hunted." He turned to glare at Sarah. "You should be hunting God for all of his crimes against humanity. The church discriminates against all kinds of things like condom use or same-sex marriage. It's a privilege this or a privilege that." He used his finger to make a point as Sarah watched him calmly, easing her heart rate back to normal. "I'll tell you what a privilege is," he continued. "The church doesn't pay any taxes. That's a fucking privilege. Make sense to you, sister? Or are you really a nun? You look much too young to be a nun. And look what you did to my guard. Only a trained expert could kill that silently. What rival cartel are you from? Or are you some kind of exterminator with the American government?"

The odds of getting out of here alive were lowering by the second. The snake was about to bite. She had come too far, in too deep. It was time to cut the snake's head off.

She moved closer to the lieutenant.

"I want to send a message to the Enzo Cartel," she said.

He offered a large nod, a wide grin pasted to his features even though his forehead was covered in sweat that leaked into his eyes. He was afraid, but as the noise outside the restroom door intensified, he seemed to grow sure of himself. "Tell me your secrets. Confess, and you shall be absolved."

He was clearly making fun of her, secure in the notion that she was alone and could not possibly pose a threat to him. But thoughts of what they had done to Aaron in his time as their prisoner fueled anger in her. She wanted to murder every last member of the Enzo Cartel. She wanted to wipe the cartel off the map. How many kids in America would be spared cartel drugs by doing so? Was that her motivation? Or was it revenge? If so, she needed a clear head because revenge would probably get her killed. Anger would cloud her judgment and cause her to slip up. A calm, rational, unemotional way of dealing with things must prevail. She would have to fight to stay in control.

She leaned closer, the gun on her right pressing against the flesh of her thigh. Suddenly the urge to pee struck her.

"The message is from Sarah Roberts." He gasped at the mention of her name. Sarah grabbed her gun under the habit. Killing this lieutenant would send a strong message.

"Go on," he said. "And while you're at it, you can tell me how you know Sarah Roberts."

"Sarah Roberts wants you to know she's on her way to hurt the cartel."

"She's coming here?" he asked, eyebrows raised as well as his voice. "Now? This café?"

Sarah nodded, gripping the gun still covered by the habit, aimed at the lieutenant's groin.

"She said she needed to know where they were keeping Aaron. But I told her you would never give that information away for free."

"You've got to be kidding," the lieutenant said dramatically.

Something slammed into the restroom door from the hallway, and Sarah jumped. She almost squeezed the trigger and shot the lieutenant. It was only a matter of seconds before they got in.

"I'm not kidding." She lowered her voice so only he could hear her. "In fact, Sarah's here right now."

The lieutenant made a joke of looking around the restroom. Sarah leaned in far enough that the gun's barrel touched his crotch. The lieutenant glanced down, his eyes widening when he understood the position he was in.

"Where's Aaron?" Sarah asked under her breath. "Where the fuck are you people keeping him?"

He looked into her eyes. "I'll take you to him," he replied

calmly. "Simply lower the gun, and we'll go for a ride. Just the two of us."

Who did these people think they were? Why would they travel all the way to Toronto to kidnap Aaron? Why do all this? She wished the cartel had left them alone. She didn't want this war, but they had started it.

Something banged into the door again. Wood splintered. One, maybe two more hits, and the door would give way.

"The only ride you'll be taking is in a hearse." Sarah wished she could stop everything and go pee, but her bladder would have to wait. "Where's Aaron?"

He laughed, then as the laugh faded, his features hardened.

"You will be killed in this café. You will not leave it alive. Then they will kill the hostage, your boyfriend. One day your parents will come out of government protection, and we will kill them after we skin them alive. You can't win, whore. No bitch has ever bettered the cartel. Now, put that thing away, and I'll make sure your death is quick and painless—"

Something banged into the door once more. It sounded like they were inside the restroom. Maddened by the image of the severed finger the cartel had sent her, Sarah pulled the trigger twice.

At first, the lieutenant's face registered surprise, then shock as he realized he'd been shot in the crotch. When he looked down to examine the wound, Sarah fired again, this time aiming higher, near the heart.

The lieutenant slammed backward into the stall door, bounced it open, and fell inside it. The front of the stained toilet connected with his shoulder blades as he landed on the filthy floor. His head dangled back over the open toilet he hadn't flushed after using the facilities.

"There's my message," she mumbled to him. "I hope your cartel hears it loud and clear."

With a resounding crack, the restroom door splintered inward and smashed into the same wall Sarah had leaned against as she watched the guard wash his hands in the sink.

She brought her weapon up and began firing at anything that moved.

Gunfire erupted throughout the café beyond the door. She crouched by the convulsing body of the lieutenant, just inside the stall door, as men shouted beyond the restroom. Weapons fired, men grunted, and bullets met targets.

Who the hell's firing at whom? Were Casper's men here to pull her out? A rival cartel? Who?

The smell of cordite mixed with sweat permeated the restroom, becoming the dominant smell over the putrid shit smell she had been getting used to.

She edged out from behind the stall door, her gun leading the way. Someone moaned. A weapon fired somewhere. The moaning stopped.

She hadn't expected the Wild West feel of this and hated it. It was dangerous, reckless, and could get her killed. Even with Vivian, she wasn't above being murdered. But for some reason, her sister had wanted her here tonight.

The lieutenant had stopped moving behind her. Blood had pooled under him and seeped onto the nun's habit. She looked back at him and felt nothing. Cartel men were glorified murderers, rapists, and drug dealers. A few less in the world made it a better place.

She made it to the broken restroom door without being

shot at. Five bodies littered the floor just past the opening. The other two body-builder types who had been guarding the lieutenant were dead. A couple of men from the bar were also dead. Beer and bar nuts littered the floor. Blood was painted everywhere. If anyone were left, it would be the bartender. It was always the bartender.

Sarah hesitated in the corridor that led from the restroom to the main area of the café, holding her weapon in front of her two-handed.

What the hell? Who did this?

Whoever was still out there could cut her down without a moment's thought. She weighed the chances that it was Casper's people and decided it couldn't be. She was dressed in a nun's habit that she had taken from a distraught nun in a church three blocks away. No one saw her there and certainly didn't follow her here to just up and kill everyone in the joint. Whoever did this was powerful and not on her side. Since this was the only way out of the building, as the windows in the restroom were too small, she had to run for it.

Someone moved into view. She fired twice so fast that she almost lost her balance. The figure tilted sideways, bumped the wall, and fell on top of two other bodies by a broken table.

"Sarah?" A man's voice. "That you? You okay?"

He sounded American. Maybe Canadian. Her bladder was so full now she wanted to just piss in the nun's habit. It was covered in water from the floor of that rancid restroom and the blood of her victims. What would it matter? There'd be no time to sit for a pee in the next half hour anyway. She had to get back to the hotel. If Casper found her amid this slaughter, there was no telling what the Federales would do to her.

"Sarah, there's still one more. Stay where you are."

A friendly. But who? The voice was younger than Parkman's and certainly not Aaron's. It wasn't Casper, and none of the men Casper had introduced her to this past week sounded that young.

Yet there was something about the voice that was familiar.

Something thumped near the back of the café. She edged out to look around the wall. A door had just closed, swinging shut softly.

Why were there no sirens outside? There had been a lot of gunplay. Anywhere in Canada or the States, that amount of gunplay would warrant a police response unless they were told not to come, regardless of what they heard. Could the cartel have that much power? She wasn't naïve. There were bribes and officers who accepted payoffs, but whole police forces?

The man who spoke to her earlier still hadn't shown himself. The other man he said was still alive hadn't either. They were in a stalemate until someone stuck their head up. But Sarah didn't want to wait any longer. She had to leave this place. And she had to pee.

As quietly as possible, Sarah moved into the open, heading for the bar. It would provide shelter, which would get her closer to the back door. She made it to the corner of the bar uninterrupted. The base of the barstools were screwed to the floor. She placed a foot on the one closest to her, looked around one last time, then lifted herself up and stepped onto the bar. Standing this high made a huge target of herself, but walking through the café to get around the lengthy bar would leave her in the open for much more time.

She bent over, kicked her feet off the bar, and hopped down behind it like dropping into a trench.

"Don't move," a man said. "Don't even flinch."

Sarah froze. The bartender was hunched in a corner, blood running from his mouth. He was wounded but alive. And he held a rather large shotgun on her.

"Drop the weapon and the knife," he said. "Easy now."

Sarah held both weapons up and out and made a show of dropping them.

"Now kick them away."

She did it, then turned back to the bartender.

"Is this about me not paying for my drink?" she asked. "Because I can gladly pay for my drink."

"What? No. Who are you?"

"Sister Margarita. I've come to offer these fine folks their last rites."

"You knew"—he coughed—"they were going to be slaughtered?" Blood covered the hand that caught the cough.

She faced him. "I had a feeling. A premonition." Her hand slipped down and gripped the last weapon strapped to her leg, her second and only gun.

"Did this premonition warn you of your own death?"

"No, can't say that it did. It said I'd make it out alive. Funny how those things work, eh?" She smiled.

He raised the shotgun to the point she was sure he was about to shoot, then got lost in a fit of coughing.

She flipped the safety off the gun under the habit, and instead of pulling it out of its holster and getting it caught in the fabric of the habit, she dropped to her butt, aimed with her knee, and squeezed the trigger before his coughing stopped.

The first bullet went wide and startled the bartender. He adjusted his shotgun, made to fire, and then a huge boom filled the café.

Sarah tried to fire again, but her finger snagged in the fabric. She scrunched her eyes closed, ducked back, and waited for the pain.

But the pain didn't come. She opened her eyes. Half of the bartender's face was missing. She looked down at the impression of her weapon under the habit. She hadn't fired again.

Who shot the bartender?

"Sarah, we need to finish this and leave."

"Who's we?" she shouted from her position on the floor behind the bar.

"I've come a long way to save your ass."

Something reeked of gasoline. The smell overwhelmed the stench of alcohol and blood.

"The least you could do is come and give me a hug before I burn this café to the ground."

The familiarity of the voice came to her. But it couldn't be. All the way from Italy? How did he know where to find her? Why did he come?

She leaned sideways to pick up the gun and the knife the bartender made her drop, then grabbed the edge of the bar to get to her feet.

Cautiously, she peeked over the edge of the bar. When she saw who he was, she stood to her full height.

"Darwin Kostas?" she asked as a warm glow enveloped her. "I don't understand."

He was dumping the contents of a red canister on the

floorboards by the front wall. Earlier, he'd worn a balaclava. That was when she'd come out of the restroom and shot him twice.

"The one and only."

"But I shot you."

"And it still hurts." He stopped dumping the canister, tossed it aside, and met her eyes. "Kevlar." He smiled. "Do you ever look different as a nun." He waved a hand for her to join him. "Come on. We have to leave."

Sarah clambered over the bar. "Where are we going?"

Darwin and his wife had virtually saved her life in Italy and then again in Toronto after she'd been shot in the head a while back. To see him here warmed her heart. To show up when she needed him the most was like a gift from God. He was trim, fit, and even a little buff. He'd lost weight and appeared to have been working out. Darwin had been through a lot—tortured by two Italian mafia families and then the Bratva, the Russian mafia—and had the scars to prove it. But now, in his early thirties, he and his wife had retired to the green hills of Umbria, Italy, where he acted like a one-man NSA, monitoring chatter, gathering data, and watching the mafia in case his name came up. He would not be surprised by them ever again. Sarah was sure if Darwin ever got wind the mafia was coming for him, he would attack first, swift and hard and in a way that would cripple their efforts and destroy their motivation. It was better if things just stayed quiet. Better for the mafia.

"We're going to my cabin," Darwin said. "To regroup. To figure things out. Then we pounce and get Aaron."

Sarah landed on the floor on the other side of the bar and started toward him. "Okay. But I have, like, a thousand questions."

"We'll have lots of time for that, but first, we have to raze this place."

She ran up and hugged him, a tear in her eye. "I'm so glad to see a friendly face."

"Okay, Sarah, we'll do all this over a glass of fine wine back at the camp."

She let go and stepped back, surveying the carnage. "Burn the bastards. Send a message."

"My thoughts exactly."

"No one lives."

Darwin leaned down and applied the flame to the benzene-soaked floorboards, then retreated as flames shot up and licked the walls.

Sarah followed him outside and stopped when she saw the vehicle he'd arrived in. It was the H2 Hummer that had cruised by the front and later the back of the building before she'd entered.

"You were following me?"

"I've been watching you since you came to Italy to fight those GMO bastards. I sent that ambulance in Toronto to get you away from that sick woman and her daughter. And I didn't forget how you treated my friends who volunteered to handle the ambulance." He walked around the hood of the Hummer and stopped before entering. "And now I fly in from Rome to see if you need help, enter a café shoot out, and get shot by you twice." He smiled so wide his teeth showed. "Is there a chance you could *stop* showing me how much you appreciate my help?"

He hopped in the Hummer as a smile broke out on Sarah's face. She got in on her side just as Darwin dropped the transmission into drive and hit the gas. The powerful V-8 shot the beast of a vehicle forward. They didn't get twenty yards before the windows of the café blew out.

"How did you shoot the bartender back there? He was crouched behind the bar."

"I located him by his voice."

Sarah raised her eyebrows in surprise. "Wow, impressive."

"Practice."

"Why are you here?"

He glanced sidelong at her. "I hacked EPIC."

"EPIC? What's that?"

"El Paso Intelligence Center. It's a database of information that comes from the DEA and Immigration and Customs. According to them, nothing was going to be done about Aaron."

Sarah twisted sideways in the passenger seat. "What are you talking about?"

Darwin stole a glance at her, then back at the road. "There are undercover agents, multiple agencies monitoring the cartels, and hundreds of people working a thousand angles on as many cases. They have been ordered to not upset the balance for one man. In this case, that one man is Aaron Stevens."

Sarah tightened her fists. "I'm going to kill Casper."

"You mean Buck Schaffer?"

"The same."

"He had nothing to do with this. They hadn't told him yet. As far as I can tell, tonight was your last night in Mexico. You and your team at the hotel were going to be ordered out of Mexico later this morning." He paused. "Without Aaron.

So I got prepared as I didn't think you would go quietly. I had a feeling Vivian would have something to say about it, too."

Sarah looked out and watched the passing landscape. Darwin gave her a moment.

"You'll have to tell me how you came to learn all this," Sarah said. "I'd love to know just half of what you can do."

"Rosina is still back in Italy at the house. She's our liaison on this. She's feeding me intel. I was watching the hotel and saw you run down the back in the dark. Infrared glasses, although they're green, not red. Anyway, I watched you enter the church, then saw a nun leave. I quickly surmised it was you, but you'd found a hiding spot near the café, so I drove around trying to reacquire you. By the time you were being attacked in the bathroom, I had to take out the men in the front room." He shrugged one shoulder. "I couldn't let them harm you, now could I?" He cleared his throat. "It was pretty easy as they all aimed their attention at the back of the café. And you know I have no compunction with that kind of wholesale murder, providing it's mafia or cartel men."

Sarah nodded her understanding. She had been followed by a fucking Hummer and didn't catch it. Was she losing some of her edge?

"Sarah, you were being lied to," Darwin added. "They're going to leave Aaron here. I couldn't let that happen." He reached across and tapped her shoulder with his palm. "We'll find him. We'll get him out."

"Where are we going first?" Sarah asked.

"The hotel. Talk to Casper. Get your things. Then I'm taking you to a safe house just outside Tijuana. A cabin. I have wine. You'll have your own room and bathroom. It'll be our retreat until this is over."

"Good, because even if Casper didn't know they were pulling the rug out on this, he should have."

"Don't hurt him too badly."

"I won't. Not too bad." She glanced at Darwin. "But just a little."

Darwin dropped the pedal farther, and the Hummer shot forward with great speed, bouncing along the Mexican road, making her bladder scream.

She still had to pee.

Chapter 4

Parkman stood in the kitchen of the safe house and looked around with a blank stare, dismayed at his position.

There were no fucking toothpicks to be had anywhere. Even after he'd specifically requested they be brought in. Not a single piece of shit toothpick.

He rifled through the drawers, going through utensils, forks, knives, spoons, shoving oven mitts, scissors, and plastic wrap out of the way but to no avail. No toothpicks.

Until he found wooden skewer sticks.

Triumphant, he stood with them in his hand, slipped one out, and snapped it in half.

From somewhere in the house, he heard a heavy groan. Then nothing.

Parkman looked down the hallway toward the living room, where the TV played a car commercial. Fred King was the agent inside the house, and Kira Junod was outside. The third agent remained on the other side of the perimeter, watching from afar. Parkman remembered her name as Special Agent Ellen Burns. A strong woman who spoke little.

Was it the TV that had emitted that moan? Or Fred?

He slipped the skewer piece between his lips and started down the hall to where he'd left Fred not five minutes ago in search of toothpicks.

A new commercial blasted out of the TV speakers talking about panty liners with wings and how they were super absorbent.

With instincts honed after years of police work and now detective work, Parkman's radar began pinging. He calculated that something was wrong in seconds because Fred hated commercials. Fred complained that the Hollywood People—as he put it—had found a way to raise the volume when commercials came on the screen, so Fred muted every commercial. But these weren't muted. Fred King would never let that happen. If Fred was anything, he was disciplined, and commercials had no place in his life. The fact that they were on meant Fred was incapacitated in some way or not in the living room any longer.

But if he'd left the room, why? To go where? Agent Junod was outside, and Agent Burns was further still. Shift change was set for seven in the morning, not one in the morning.

Parkman waited at the alcove that led into the living room, took a few deep breaths, and listened to the house. He was rewarded with nothing. Slipping the skewer from one side of his mouth to the other, he turned and glanced into the living room.

Agent King, or Fred as he had ordered Parkman to call

him, sat in his armchair, head back, snoring.

He'd fallen asleep? On the job?

Parkman examined the room with a trained eye. Nothing appeared disturbed. The coffee table was as he'd left it, a mess. The remote was still in Fred's hand. There were no depressions in the carpet, no marks. Nothing to suggest someone had entered the house.

Then Fred snored a short, sharp grunt.

That was probably what Parkman had heard moments before.

He moved closer to Fred, still examining the room for anything untoward. Then he eased the remote out of Fred's grip and muted the TV.

A radio emitted a female voice. Fred's radio.

Parkman found the radio inside Fred's duffel bag. He brought it to his ear and listened. It was Agent Burns. She was running, her breath coming in and out in gasps.

And she was calling for Fred to respond.

Parkman depressed the button. "Parkman here," he whispered. "What's your twenty?"

"Ten seconds out."

"What happened?"

"Shadowy figures approached the house. I almost didn't see them. Two, three, maybe more. Where's Agent King?"

"Asleep in the armchair."

"Shit!"

"What?"

"He's not asleep. King never sleeps. Too disciplined."

Parkman looked back at Fred. Slight discoloration had formed at the base of his neck. Someone had choked him, knocked him out. They probably stopped when Parkman approached from the kitchen. Probably choked Fred as Parkman made all that noise with the utensils looking for toothpicks. Parkman wouldn't have heard a damn thing.

"You're right. He's been strangled by the looks of it, but he's alive."

"Shit!"

"What now?" Parkman asked as he lowered himself to the carpet, removed Fred's ankle-holstered gun, and moved to the wall to offer less of a target of himself to the intruders.

"Agent Junod is out cold," Burns whispered into the radio.

Parkman took this information in stride. Whoever was attacking the safe house was good, efficient, and meant to take him. But for some reason, they weren't killing the federal agents, which was a good thing. He'd hate to have their lives on his hands.

"Agent Burns, watch your back. I'm covered. I'm safe. Take care of yourself."

There was no response.

"Agent Burns? Come in."

Nothing.

A weapon fired outside the front window. He wondered if she had already called for backup and how long backup would take at one in the morning. Calling backup to a house that, by definition, is secret is always challenging. Local authorities never know how to respond to a suburban house suddenly becoming a hot spot for guns. They never know who the bad guys are because everyone has weapons.

Another weapon discharged outside, this time beside the house, right behind the wall where Parkman rested his back.

He placed an ear against the drywall and listened. A male

voice mumbled something. Another male answered. It sounded like he said he was happy to have finished off the last bitch with so many bullets.

Parkman's stomach dropped, and his bowels loosened in fear and anticipation. Could this be it? Trapped in a plastic house without toothpicks, three agents down? Attacked by a rogue gang, an extension of the Enzo Cartel hunting Sarah? A cold sweat broke out on his forehead and the back of his neck. The hand that held Fred's gun shook, but not enough that he'd miss what he shot at. Professional or not, fear of the unknown still shook him up.

He pushed his ear into the wall harder, trying to catch anything they said. He waited, listening.

The floor creaked beside him. Before he turned, before he responded, his gun hand was rising, then it was knocked sideways with such extreme violence, Fred's gun was torn from his grasp.

He swung his head around, gasped at the pain in his hand, and locked in on the man in black standing over him.

Fred's gun had sailed over the TV and was too far to get to. Parkman was unarmed unless he could use the skewer to jab the guy to death.

"On your feet, Parkman," the black figure shouted. "We're taking you to Mexico."

Chapter 5

WHEN CASPER WOKE, HIS head was splitting with a migraine from hell. He winced, squeezed his eyes closed, and rested his head back down. Something rough like straw or scattered hay was his bed. Casper tried to remember and categorize his last thoughts as his stomach threatened to clench and dislodge its contents. What led him here, wherever here was? He took a mental inventory of his body and discovered it to be intact. Nothing ached but his head.

The hotel. The waiting. He tried to raise Sarah on the phone. Her room was empty. The guard by the elevator was dead. The tranquilizer. The cartel.

They had him.

If the cartel had him, he was as good as dead. There was no way they'd let a federal agent live. He'd be tortured for information, used for negotiation, maybe even a prisoner-for-ransom scheme, then killed, his body dumped on a roadside somewhere.

He had failed. He had failed Sarah. Had he been overconfident? Was his mistake arrogance? Who tipped off the cartel? Someone in the hotel? The Federales? Was there no justice, no laws, no respect for authority in Mexico? He should've known better. A whole week in the hotel made them sitting targets. Of course, the Enzo Cartel would learn of their presence soon enough. That many rooms taken up by the American authorities was like a large marquee sign announcing their presence.

It was all for show. The Mexican government allowed it and kept them waiting. That had to be it. Otherwise, why not wait for the red tape to be cleared on American soil in San Diego? It would've been safer on the American side. How many agents were lost? All of them?

A tear crested his eyelid and slid down into his ear. *What now*, he thought as the tear cooled in his ear. How long did he have to live? How long did Sarah have to live?

"You awake?" a man asked.

Casper started and tried to open his eyes. "Who's there?"

"You first."

"Special Agent Buck Schaffer, also known as Casper. You?"

"Casper, eh? You supposed to be a ghost?"

The accent wasn't American. But it wasn't Mexican either. It sounded Canadian. In all likelihood, he was talking to Aaron.

Casper finally got his eyes open to slits and turned toward the voice. Aaron Stevens sat in the corner of a small room, legs drawn up to his chest, hands wrapped around his legs. His right hand had a large, bloodstained bandage wrapped around it.

Casper eased his head back and shut his eyes. "I'm sorry, Aaron."

A sudden movement in the corner. "You know me?"

"I'm the one in charge of locating and extracting you."

The scrambling stopped. It sounded like Aaron settled back down.

"Great. There goes that idea."

"Yeah. Sorry."

Neither spoke for a few moments. Casper focused on his breathing, hoping the wretched headache would dissipate.

"What's that fetid smell?"

"Hector."

"Who's Hector?"

"An employee who allegedly stole from these guys. He was beaten and then murdered in this prison cell. Left to rot. They just removed him a few days back."

"Hmmph, sounds like nice enough fellows."

"Yeah, real classy joint."

Casper breathed deeply. Aaron huddled silently.

"What next?" Aaron asked a few minutes later.

"We get you out."

"How? Was getting captured part of your plan?"

"No, but I'm adaptable. Now that I'm inside their compound, I've done half my job. I've found you. The other half is getting you out."

"You can't. Security is too tight. There's got to be a hundred men on the grounds. The electric fence is topped with barbed wire. Signs say High Voltage."

"You've been outside?" Casper asked, his attitude becoming more positive.

"A few times on occasion when they drag me to the barn for water torture and finger cutting."

"Tell me about the outside. Paint a picture."

"There's no use. Unless you can fly a helicopter, you'll never escape this place. It's a virtual prison."

"I don't want to escape it."

"Then what does it matter?"

"You're going to escape. And I've got an idea how. Now, shut up about it and describe everything you saw in fine detail. I want to know it all, see it all. Got it?"

Aaron shuffled something on his side of the room, made a thumping noise, then began talking.

Soon, Casper saw the outside of the prison walls while his eyes remained closed, and he waited for the headache to subside.

Chapter 6

SARAH EASED UP FROM a prone position to sit on the couch. Darwin stood at the stove in the kitchen on the other side of the cabin. The smell of eggs, bacon, and toast wafted Sarah's way. Her stomach yearned for nourishment. The shit they'd fed her at the hotel was clogging her system up, but Casper had professed they had to eat hotel food or risk getting some kind of illness. Especially the water. It had to be bottled water. Sarah had asked about the ice. What water did the hotel use to make ice? Casper hadn't answered her. She didn't have ice in any of her drinks.

"Morning," Darwin said.

"Hey." She rubbed the sleep from her eyes.

"You always sleep that good after a few murders?" he asked.

"What? Those guys? I hate sounding cliché, but I don't lose sleep over scum."

"Good. Me neither. Get up, use the bathroom, then come to the table. Breakfast's ready."

"What's the hurry?"

"We have a lot to talk about. Then we need to make a move."

Sarah headed for the toilet. The same toilet she finally got to use last night when they arrived after leaving the carnage at the Baja Café behind. When Darwin approached the hotel where Casper and his men had been keeping Sarah, the road was blocked and rerouted. They had gotten close enough to see four ambulances and at least a dozen police cars, marked and unmarked, surrounding the front. Some kind of attack had taken place in her absence. She only hoped Casper was still alive and the casualties were minimal.

When she was done in the bathroom, she emerged to a steaming breakfast on the table and a smiling Darwin in his chair, waiting for her to join him.

"How did you get your name again?" she asked as she pulled her chair out.

"My name? You mean, Darwin?"

Sarah nodded and sat down.

"Survival of the fittest. My father was Greek, hence the last name Kostas, even though that's usually a first name in Greece."

Sarah got comfortable and dug into her food.

"Thanks for this," she said between bites. "Much needed."

"No problem," he said. "Nourishment is as much an ally as any weapon when fighting an enemy. One must be at their maximum physical potential at all times."

She stopped chewing and looked up at him. "You sound

like you're putting on a seminar."

He bit into his bacon and watched her as he chewed without responding.

"Sorry," she said. "That sounded rude and ungrateful."

"Don't worry. I don't take things personally. The world doesn't revolve around me. I'm the one who has to adapt and learn to live inside the world. Comments like that flatter me."

Sarah removed the whites from around her yolks, then took the yolk intact into her mouth, squeezed it with her tongue until it burst, and fought off the urge to moan.

"Interesting way to eat eggs," Darwin commented.

She swallowed. "I've always loved the intensity of a bursting yolk, flooding my mouth with its richness." She swallowed again. "What do we have to talk about?"

"Bad news." Darwin's face soured. "I heard from Rosina."

Sarah set her fork down. "Has something happened to your wife?"

"No, nothing like that. She's been monitoring everything from Italy and giving me hourly updates."

"What has she discovered?" Sarah asked as she picked up a strip of bacon and bit into it.

"The safe house Parkman was being held at was hit last night."

Sarah dropped her bacon. It missed the plate and landed on the tablecloth.

"What?"

"Whoever did it was extremely professional, but they're not sure who it was yet."

"What can you tell me?"

"Three agents, two outside, one inside. All were subdued

and knocked out. No sign of Parkman. No sign of blood."

Sarah frowned. "That doesn't sound like cartel men. With a chance to take out federal agents, they'd take it. They kill cops down here in Mexico just to send a message."

Darwin nodded. "I once read a cartel boss's statement that cartels don't kill for money. They don't kill women, innocents, or children. They only kill those who *should* die. The problem with that is they're the ones who determine who should die. Which could be all of the above."

"Twisted."

They stared at each other a moment longer until Darwin nodded. Sarah started in on her breakfast again, not knowing when the next time would be when she would get to eat something so tasty.

Darwin continued. "There's been no sign of Parkman. Customs at the border are on high alert. His description has been circulated to every point of entry in California."

"Why just California?"

"He was being contained in San Diego, right close to the border, in case they needed to get him into Mexico fast to help with you, as far as I understand it. With him being that close, whoever took him, if they intend to bring him down here, they'll try to sneak him in immediately. They may already have. The window of opportunity closed fast in the middle of the night. Today it would be much harder."

Sarah wiped the rest of her plate clean with the toast Darwin had piled on a plate in the center of the table.

"Thanks for this," Sarah said.

"You don't seem too concerned for Parkman. Or am I reading you wrong?"

Sarah leaned back in her chair, stretched, and waited to

respond until her mouth was clear. "He's fine wherever he is. Vivian's close by. I can feel her. I can feel her emotional state. She's not talking right now, but she knows about Parkman and is okay with it. So I am, too."

Darwin looked stunned. "You've changed."

"I'm a new person since you last saw me in Italy. After I got shot in the head … it was like a portal opened. Vivian can access me directly now. It took some getting used to and a small learning curve, but now she just talks to me. She's so close I can feel her emotions, and the best part is, she can translate better than any app."

"What?" Darwin said, eyebrows raised, mouth open.

"When I was in Greece, as the taxi driver spoke to me in Greek, a language I know nothing about, Vivian whispered what he said and then told me how to answer in Greek. When I hear the language in my head, it rolls off my tongue almost accent free." She could tell this news was shocking Darwin. "Chinese too."

"Chinese!" he shouted.

"Yeah," she shrugged. Wanting to change the subject, she said, "What else did Rosina tell you?"

Darwin drank the rest of his orange juice, set the cup down, and got up from the table. He started to clear the dishes.

"Last night's hit on the hotel you were staying at was the Enzo Cartel, according to the authorities."

Sarah looked down at her napkin and began fiddling with it. How close did she come to being taken by them in the hotel full of DEA, FBI, CIA, and every other alphabet acronym she could come up with?

"How many dead?" she asked, knowing the cartel

wouldn't have just knocked the authorities out and left them all sleeping.

"Thirty dead. But the media isn't releasing that number."

Her stomach felt like a pit of ore. The food rolled around in an attempt to be digested, but her nerves forced acid into the mix, upsetting the balance.

"Did Rosina get access to a list of names?"

"If you're referring to Special Agent Buck Schaffer, he's been reported as missing from the scene."

"Missing?" Sarah snapped, looking up at Darwin.

Darwin set the plates on the counter. "They're assuming he was kidnapped."

Hopelessness settled in over her system. Aaron had been gone for almost two weeks now. Parkman was missing. Casper had been kidnapped. Darwin and Rosina were the only good things to come out of all this. Without them, she might have been killed last night in her recklessness. But, of course, Vivian knew about Darwin. Otherwise, she wouldn't have sent her after the lieutenant.

"What now?" Sarah asked. "I don't even know where this cartel is or how they operate. We were supposed to rely on intel from the Mexican authorities, but they weren't very forthcoming."

She got up and moved to the couch, stretching out to rest her stomach.

Darwin took the chair facing her.

"I've researched the Enzo Cartel and cartels in general. They control ninety percent of the cocaine entering the U.S." Darwin leaned back and cleared his throat. "Wholesale earnings are as high as fifty billion a year. Some of the cartels near border towns like Tijuana have taken over trafficking cocaine from Columbia by working with FARC."

"I've heard that name. Remind me who they are again."

"It stands for Las Fuerzas Armadas Revolucionarias de Colombia. Last I read, they were nearly a 20,000-strong army in Columbia. Anyway, all the cocaine from Columbia, Peru, and Ecuador runs through them in an exchange for guns program."

"They sound bigger and more organized than the mafia."

"In some ways, they are. They're involved in kidnapping, ransom, murder, robbery, and extortion, just like the mafia. But they are always trying to find new and unique ways to kill and inspire fear in their enemies. And they have no issue with killing cops, unlike the mafia. They also launder money like the mafia, but cartels are known to launder over forty billion dollars through the United States annually."

Sarah rested her arm over her forehead. "What does all this mean for Aaron? Where is he, and how can I get him out?"

"I've got an idea for that."

She glanced his way. "What's your idea?"

"You call the DEA office in San Diego and offer up something tasty for them."

"What does that mean?" Sarah sat on the edge of her chair.

"Tell them where the Enzo Cartel is meeting or where a pick up is taking place. Hurt them. Get some of their members arrested or even killed. Do this a few times in a row."

"How am I supposed to know that kind of information? If I knew where they were, *I'd* go after them."

"You have to ask your sister. But here's my point. We

have to rattle them. Then we take you to the hospital."

She reared back. "Hospital?" He wasn't making sense. "Why would I go to a hospital?"

"To arm a gurney with explosives and guns."

"And do what with it?"

"Now, this is the good part." He licked his lips and rubbed his hands together. "I want you to get kidnapped by the Enzo Cartel. Go inside armed to the teeth. Find Aaron. And prepare for my assault. I'll be tracking you the entire time with GPS. It's the only way to find their compound. Even the Mexican authorities have no clue where the cartel's headquarters are. Enzo wants you. The cartel guys will take you to their camp. Once you're inside, they won't kill you fast. That'll give me time to get in and take them all out."

"Gee, thanks. Not kill me fast. Why am I not liking this idea too much yet?" Sarah looked down at the cabin's hardwood floor. As crazy as this idea sounded, there was something that made sense to it. She looked back up. "I can grow to like it. But how are you—one man—going to enter a cartel compound and save the day?"

"I won't be one man. I have about a dozen fully trained mercenaries at my disposal."

"Mercs? A dozen? How?"

"I've been slowly recruiting since I've been in Italy in the event that I end up having another showdown with the mafia. I've worked with these men, trained with them, and offered a number of them refuge when they needed it. At the back of my property, I dug out a subterranean floor. We train underground, out of sight of satellites and curious onlookers. Now I'm calling in favors. I've called all twelve. At least seven are entering Mexico over the next several days. None of them can be bought by a cartel. In this part of the world, they are loyal only to me." His chest swelled as he spoke of these men. "I've handpicked them for this assignment."

"This sounds like a scene from Expendables. You've got to be kidding."

Darwin shook his head back and forth.

"And you're doing this for me?" Sarah asked. "So I can get Aaron out?"

He nodded.

"Why?"

"Because one day you'll return the favor. Maybe even save my life. But I don't do it for a return. I do it because it's who I am now. It's what I do best. And I hate organized groups of criminals. The mafia, a cartel, they're all the same to me."

"I don't know what to say." Sarah got up from the table and approached the large window that looked out on the Mexican terrain.

"Say you'll agree to be a chunk of bait," Darwin said. "It's the only way I can think of getting you inside. Eventually, they'll kidnap you anyway. Better it's on our terms."

"Great. Thanks for that." She smiled. "You're right. Let's rattle their cage, then set me up to be taken." She turned from the window with thoughts of Aaron, Parkman, and Casper on her mind. This was no time to be idle. They had to attack viciously, hard, and fast.

Darwin clapped his hands. "I'll set things in motion and get the gear prepared. You talk to Vivian and get me whatever you can on the cartel. Then we go after them."

Sarah moved to the couch. On her way across the floor,

Vivian left her consciousness. It felt like an eagle gently, quietly falling off a tree's high perch. When she did that, Sarah felt a void open inside. The void was filled with despair and dread.

Vivian moved away when she wanted no part in something.

Vivian moved away when she disapproved.

There would be no cartel locations, no assignments for the DEA to rattle the Enzo cage. Vivian wasn't willing to offer anything unless she deemed it necessary. She could never be told what to do. Sarah understood that. And hated it.

Pushing Vivian never worked. Her sister talked when her sister was ready to talk.

It reminded Sarah of someone very close to her.

Vivian reminded Sarah of herself.

Chapter 7

THE PRISON DOOR OPENED a crack. A chunk of something wrapped in aluminum foil was shoved inside, and the door jerked closed, secured from the outside.

Casper crawled over and unwrapped the package.

"Two buns with butter," he said. He met Aaron's eyes. "Why the butter? A female's touch, perhaps? Why not just the bread?"

Aaron shrugged. "It's better than the one bun yesterday."

Casper crawled closer to Aaron and handed him the package.

"Here, you eat both."

Aaron snapped his head up. "What? Why?"

"You need to get your strength up."

"And you don't?"

"You're the martial arts expert. You're the hand-to-hand combat guru. My physical state will decline over the next few days without food, but I need yours healing. At least meet me halfway. Eat all the food they give us for a week, and then if we're still alive in a week, I'll start eating my share."

"Absolutely not." Aaron shoved a bun in front of Casper. "Eat your share now."

Casper stared into Aaron's eyes. "I wasn't joking. Get your strength up. Eat. You need to survive this. It's you they want, not me. I'm a federal agent. I'll probably be dead inside twenty-four hours."

"Don't be ridiculous. Why would they kill you?"

"You're being naïve. This is a Mexican cartel. After what they did to Hector, you think they'll let a federal agent live? Eating that food would be wasting it. Now eat. Then do pushups and sit-ups. Build your strength. Be ready. That's how you survive this."

Casper crawled away and sat in the farthest corner from Aaron as he ate. How long had he been unconscious? How far from Tijuana were they? And how did the Mexican authorities not know about this place?

His personal items had been taken. His ring, watch, and wallet had been removed. Even his socks and shoes. They must have taken it to incinerate it. To begin the process of removing any sign of Special Agent Buck Schaffer. He had to admit to himself that this was the end. He had sat in that hotel as if in a thick web, waiting for the spider to claim its prize. He had made mistakes before and underestimated people, but this was by far the dumbest mistake he'd ever made, and it would cost him his life.

His long and illustrious career had two black marks, which were circumstantial errors. Early in his career, his partner had been ambushed, shot, and killed at a house fire. They had been responding to shots fired in the area. When they got there, the house was ablaze. Rick stayed out front while Casper ran to the back. He was able to crawl in a broken window and pull out an unconscious five-year-old boy. He had saved the boy's life, but his partner had died. The house owner had just killed his wife and was trying to burn the evidence. When he saw a cop on his front lawn, he shot him. If the roles had been switched, Casper would've been killed. Losing a partner that way had stung. Saving the boy was the one reason Casper stayed on and dealt with Rick's death.

The other time was when he lost his cool on a female pimp during a human trafficking sting. This woman had been torturing and terrorizing her girls, some as young as fifteen, to do terrible and horrific things for the male clientele. When she was arrested, she spit in Casper's face, then head-butted him. He cuffed her in the head so hard he knocked her out. After a day in the hospital, the charges against her were dropped, and Casper was reassigned.

A year later, he heard that she had been supposedly killed by one of her own girls. No one ever proved it. The pimp's body was nearly decapitated. No weapon was ever found. No fibers, no hair, and no signs of struggle. She just ended up dead.

He'd dealt with small-time made men, hitmen, murderers, and even one serial killer case. But cartel business was his new assignment, and fucking up this early held its price.

He lowered his head and closed his eyes. A lingering effect from the tranquilizer dart made him feel drowsy. Or maybe he was just tired.

Someone smashed the exterior door. Chains rattled outside.

Casper jerked his head up. Aaron had been lying down and getting up, too. The food was nowhere in sight.

A stab of sunshine shot through the small prison cell as the door was opened.

"Get up. Let's go."

Six burly men entered the room. Two grabbed Aaron, and two came for Casper.

Is this it?

Once he was on his feet and turned toward the door, he squinted at the bright sun. They half dragged, half walked him outside, and then turned to the left. He tried to look behind him to see Aaron, but each time he did, the man on that side jammed Casper's shoulder, forcing his head straight.

The sweltering heat outside was a vast difference from the air inside the sheltered cell. From the sun's position, he put it at about ten in the morning.

Sweat broke out on the back of his neck as he struggled to keep up with the men on either side. No one said a thing, which allowed him to follow Aaron's progress behind him.

They headed across the property toward a large helicopter parked on a helipad out front of the huge house that Aaron had described earlier. The rest of the grounds were just as Aaron had said. The stables, the horses, the barn, and even the cars parked in front of the estate home.

Casper listened for traffic and cars on a highway. He searched the sky for planes. Maybe he'd see a flight path and be able to determine where Tijuana's airport was. But there was only the noise the men made. He could be at a ranch in

Maine, Montana, or New Orleans for all he knew. It certainly didn't look like Mexico. As Aaron had said, the outer fence was high, wrapped in barbed wire, and electrified.

The fence was put in after, which probably meant this estate was purchased for cartel use because the fence was built in a zig-zag formation, keeping under the shelter of tall tree branches the entire time. The fence would be hardly visible from the air. Even low-flying planes wouldn't be able to see it. These guys were serious thinkers. Whoever ran security for Enzo Miguel Guzman knew what he was doing. Unless this was Enzo's idea, which would make more sense knowing what Casper knew of the man.

As they neared the helicopter, he got a better look inside the craft. Two men were tied to the rear wall by their wrists. Bruises, welts, and lacerated skin dominated their faces, necks, and hands.

Where were they taking them? A new prison? To meet Enzo?

The benefit for him was he would get an aerial view of the estate, which would make it better to advise Aaron on his escape plans.

At the helicopter's open door, the men shoved him inside. Aaron followed, landing on the back of Casper's legs. He grunted in pain and waited until Aaron rolled off him.

Before Casper had a chance to get up, someone dragged him to the back wall, where he was secured between the two other prisoners. Aaron was tied beside him.

The rotors began spinning. Two of the men who brought him and Aaron to the helicopter jumped on board, one guarding each side's open door. They clipped into a safety hook that connected to a body harness and leaned out over the edge at a forty-five-degree angle. Each man smiled like they were kids about to take the ultimate roller coaster ride.

Moments before the helicopter lifted off, a thick man approached the open door and stared at Casper.

Aaron stiffened beside him.

"That's the man," Aaron said loud enough to be heard over the rotors. "He cut my finger off. I call him Spanish."

The man hopped on the craft, and it lifted off. He hooked himself onto a clip that ran the length of the helicopter's roof, allowing him to walk back and forth without falling out either open door.

No one spoke as the chopper cleared the main house and continued to rise, wind buffeting them from both sides. Casper caught a glimpse of the hard-packed earth and baked terrain surrounding the compound before the man—Spanish —kicked him in the side of the ribs. He buckled inward and brought his knees up.

"Why are you here, in Mexico?" Spanish shouted in his ear from a few feet away. With the doors open on either side and without a helmet, the sound of the rotors was like being in front of the speakers at a Metallica concert while the drummer thrashed on the drums repeatedly. Casper shook his head back and forth to try to block the sound of the thunderous roar.

Spanish bent down close to Casper. "Where's Sarah?" he asked. "Tell me, and I'll let you live." He leaned closer. "We'll fly by, observe Sarah, verify you're telling the truth, and then drop you off and wait for your people to pick you up." The chopper banked to the right and soared above the treetops. "Do we have a deal?"

Casper turned to face Spanish. "I have no idea where

Sarah is. She was in room 510 at the hotel. When your guys showed up, she was already gone."

"Bullshit."

Spanish stepped away, moved to one of the two men hooked to the back wall, and snapped the clip that bound him there. He fell in a heap on the chopper's floor, grasping at the floor for something to hold onto, his face panic-stricken at the thought of falling out.

Spanish shouted something to the pilot.

The helicopter flipped sideways.

Completely sideways. The prisoner groveling on the floor, disappeared out the open door and fell hundreds of feet to his death.

Spanish and his two men shot into the open air, their safety straps and harnesses supporting them as they hung there. The guard outside the helicopter was at least five feet out in the open air, smiling as he dangled from his safety strap.

The three men, still strapped to the back wall, were suspended by their cuffed wrists. Casper forced his mouth closed at the pain as Aaron, and the other prisoner screamed over the sound of the rotors.

The helicopter righted, and everyone dropped back onto the floor, minus the one man.

"One down," Spanish shouted at Casper. "The untied man fell to his death a thousand feet below because of you. Where have your people stashed Sarah?"

Casper shot a glance at Aaron and was surprised to not see the fear on his face. Aaron's jaw was set, his eyes ablaze with anger. He stared at Spanish with a mask of hatred. Casper understood that anger. He'd felt it before. Learning how to control that kind of anger was the key. Lashing out and losing your cool was a mistake, and Aaron was youthful and close to being killed for his rage. But what Casper knew of Aaron and Sarah, and what had happened to them because of this man, made him want to kill Spanish, too.

"Tell me," Spanish shouted. "Who attacked my men at the Baja Café? Did your team set that up?" He grabbed his safety rope and yanked it to lean in closer to Casper. "What does *no one lives* mean? That was the message we were supposed to receive. A nun delivered it. A nun named Sarah Roberts."

Casper averted his eyes. Sarah? Dressed as a nun? Of course. She could get inside a café and out again dressed like that.

He tried to empty his mind. His blank stare fixed on the horizon as he listened to the thunder of the rotors above.

"Tell me who drove the black Hummer. Was it your people? Or Sarah's? Whoever it was murdered a lot of my men." Spanish appeared to be losing control. "I want names," he shouted.

Spanish's helper unhooked the other prisoner as he cried and pleaded. Then he shoved him toward Spanish. The man dropped at Spanish's feet and began pleading for his life, wrapping an arm around Spanish's ankles.

Spanish drew a small pistol, leaned down, and pushed it into the top of the prisoner's head. The man's cries for mercy doubled.

"I have a hundred men scouring the streets of Tijuana looking for that fucking Hummer. It will be blasted to hell when it's found. Who drove it, *Casper*?" He said the name with obvious distaste. "Talk, Special Agent Schaffer, or this man dies."

"Don't kill him," Casper shouted. "I don't know where Sarah is, and I have no idea who was at the Baja Café. I don't know anything about a Hummer. We were ordered to stand down. We were ordered to wait. You would be killing that man for nothing."

"What does *no one lives* mean? Why send that message to me? To Enzo?"

Casper shook his head in a short spurt. "I have no idea. Maybe it was Sarah. She's on her own now. Who knows where she is." He was spewing what he could think of at the moment, but the look in Spanish's eyes told him everything. He would kill this prisoner whether he learned what he wanted to learn or not.

A second later, Spanish's eyes not leaving Casper's, he pulled the trigger.

The prisoner's body went rigid as blood shot out the other side of his head, then he dropped limp to the chopper's floor. Spanish kicked until the prisoner was gone, lost to the open air.

Casper's heart rate doubled. Spanish was certifiably insane. Firing a weapon inside the helicopter was crazy. He could have hit vital components or fuel lines, or a ricochet could kill someone. Casper could only imagine what Aaron was going through.

The helicopter changed course.

Spanish nodded toward Aaron. His beast of a guard on Aaron's side unhooked Aaron's cuffed hands and dragged him to Spanish's feet.

"Don't," Casper shouted. "You need him."

Spanish shot his head around. "I don't *need* anybody."

The wind buffeted them from both sides as the helicopter shot through the morning sky.

"What I need is the location of Sarah Roberts."

"I can't give you what you need because I don't have it."

Spanish watched him for what felt like half a minute. Then he pulled his boot back and kicked Aaron hard enough to make Aaron roll over and curl up, gasping for air.

"I don't believe you."

The helicopter leveled out, its speed tapering off. Casper thought he saw the roof of the Enzo compound's house between the trees.

"What can you tell me?" Spanish asked. "Offer something I don't already know. Spare Aaron's life."

Casper had nothing to bargain with. The Mexican authorities had kept him in the dark. He was worried he'd have to deal with an irate Sarah, and now he was being pumped for information that he didn't have. Two men had just died for nothing, and Aaron's life was next.

"Do you enjoy watching me kill people?" Spanish asked. "Is that it?"

"NO!" Casper shouted and lunged for Spanish, his cuffs stopping him well short.

Spanish leaned forward and said something to the pilot. It looked like Aaron understood what would happen and got to his knees. He met Casper's eyes. There wasn't a hint of regret in them. Just determination, fight. He was ready. But for what? Attack Spanish? He'd never succeed with the two armed men on either side.

At that moment, the helicopter flipped on its side again, and Aaron slid to the open door. At the edge, he got his feet under him and launched off the floor at the man secured by the side door. He landed on the grunt hooked up at the side door perfectly. Aaron mounted the man's shoulders like a monkey on his back. The man screamed and squirmed to dislodge Aaron, but Aaron clung tight, staring at the ground, eyes wide open.

Spanish and his other man were also helplessly suspended by their safety cords. Casper felt like his wrists would snap under the pressure. Then the chopper righted. Aaron and the man he clung to dropped to the floor of the chopper in a large heap of muscle and sweat.

Spanish was on them in seconds, driving a fist into Aaron's face twice and ripping Aaron off his man.

Casper shouted for him to stop, his voice cracking with all the yelling over the sound of the rotors.

Exhausted, Aaron rolled into the corner gasping for breath, no doubt understanding how close he came to buying the farm.

With Casper still attached to the back wall by his wrists, he was useless as Spanish, and his man brought Aaron to his feet. They stood Aaron by the helicopter's open door and walked backward, leaving him at the edge.

Spanish produced a handgun.

"Special Agent Buck Schaffer," Spanish yelled with a glance over his shoulder. "Any last words for Aaron Stevens?"

"Let him go," he yelled back. "You've got me. Just let him go. Trade me for Sarah."

"You're right. I don't need Aaron anymore. Sarah's here, in Mexico. I'll find her within days." He turned to Casper. "Did you know I have a two hundred thousand bounty on her head? Anyone who brings me her head gets a cool two hundred grand. Bring her alive, and I double it." He gestured at Aaron with the gun. "You see why I don't need him anymore?"

Aaron moved backward a few more inches. At the edge of the open doorway, a calm, resolute look fell over his face.

"I'm sorry, Casper," Aaron shouted. "But I can't be in the same room with this guy anymore, let alone the same helicopter."

"What—?" Casper shouted.

"I will never help them find Sarah. They're going to kill me anyway."

"Wait!" Casper tried again.

Spanish was smiling at this display of bravado.

"Tell Sarah I will always love her."

Casper went to yell again, but his voice cut off as Aaron fell backward out the helicopter's open door and was lost from sight.

Aaron was gone.

Spanish smiled as the machine banked away and headed back to the compound.

Casper dropped to the floor of the chopper and wept.

He whispered a silent prayer for Aaron's soul and vowed to kill Spanish for him.

Or die trying.

Chapter 8

Parkman stared out the back window of the recreational vehicle as they slowed to enter the hour-long line at the Mexican border south of San Diego.

They had stayed the night at the Travelodge and had Denny's for breakfast not a mile from the border. The eggs, ham, bacon, and pancakes that went down easy an hour before swirled in his stomach as they inched closer to border control.

He had made sure they were all apprised of the story. Just three Canadian boys, Daniel, Benjamin, and Alex, on their way to Mexico for a few days to enjoy the food, swim on the beaches and have a good time after they attend the Martial Arts Conference taking place south of Tijuana. As teachers in a Toronto school, Parkman was confident this would pass routine scrutiny. All three had up-to-date passports. As long as they stayed in character, this RV would cross the Mexican border without a problem.

Detective Folley, the man who investigated Aaron's sister's disappearance, had been pivotal in locating Parkman. When Daniel told Folley that Aaron had been kidnapped, as had Parkman and Sarah's parents, Folley did some looking into things. He called back five hours later to explain that Sarah's parents were safe and being guarded. Parkman was being held at a safe house in San Diego.

When Daniel prodded Folley on how he could know such a thing, Folley explained that it wasn't really a safe house. They kept Parkman geographically close to Mexico in case he was needed in Tijuana, minutes away on the other side of the border. A phone call to the right person, a favor used, and Folley had an address. Folley wanted to know if this favor wiped his slate clean. He felt he still owed Aaron. After Folley bungled Aaron's case and Joanne, Aaron's sister was murdered, Aaron was taken and almost killed, too; Folley always needed to make things right with Aaron. Daniel assured him they were square and that he would pass that message on to Aaron when he saw him.

Aaron's martial arts teachers had traveled to Greece to save his life. Traveling to the States to pick up Parkman and then heading to Mexico wasn't just an option, it was the only thing they could do. Sitting idly by while someone tortured Aaron made all three of them sick.

And they wanted Parkman along, who they had briefly worked with before in the past.

At the safe house, all three FBI agents were put to sleep. None of them was seriously hurt or killed. Parkman later learned the gunfire he heard outside the house was Benjamin emptying Special Agent Ellen Burns's weapon out of

them. In the end, maybe it would be him who needed the three boys. Without Sarah's talent of hearing a voice from the other side, Parkman had to go on instinct, and right now, it was telling him to go ahead, cross the border, and see where this ride took them.

"Parkman?" Daniel shouted back.

"Yeah."

"We're getting close to the border. Benjamin's coming back to settle you in."

"Okay."

Benjamin appeared in the doorway. Parkman rolled off the bed and got down on the floor. He knew what to do. They had practiced it last night.

He crawled under the bed and edged in sideways as far as he could go, the inner wall of the RV resting against his shoulder. Then Benjamin brought four duffel bags stuffed with martial arts gear down from upper cabinets and placed them in front of Parkman, shielding him from view from the inside of the trailer.

"Can you see me?" Parkman asked, the sound of his voice in the enclosed space coming back to him as if in a tunnel.

A duffel bag shoved deeper in response, butting up against his face.

"Hey, I have to be able to breathe."

"Sorry," was Benjamin's muffled response. "We're good now. They can take out two bags, but a third would expose you."

"Chances of them searching the RV are remote," Parkman yelled to him. "But if they do, let them."

"We will."

Daniel shouted something from the front, but it was lost to Parkman.

"What did he say?"

"Ten cars away. I'm heading up to my seat now."

"See you on the other side."

The dull thud of Benjamin's footsteps reverberated as Benjamin walked toward the front. Parkman breathed slowly, closed his eyes, and rested his head. This would all be over soon.

The RV edged closer. Parkman felt the movement, then the braking, and counted down one car. Maddeningly slow, Daniel pulled forward, then braked. Another car. Eight to go.

He focused on his breathing as it got stuffy, jammed up the way he was. He listened to the noises outside the RV, trying to determine what caused them. A car with a hole in its muffler drove by. Someone shouted something in Spanish about drinking too much tequila. The car behind the RV had to be close because Parkman could hear Snoop Dogg singing something about gin and juice on the stereo.

The RV moved. Was that one more or two? How close now? Five cars? Four?

The RV moved again.

Lightheaded, he dropped his head and closed his eyes. He wasn't getting enough air. Benjamin had sealed him in too tight. A cool sweat broke out on the back of his neck, and his stomach rolled with the nerves. Would he hyperventilate at such a crucial moment?

The RV moved.

He couldn't budge an inch. Pushing a bag out to breathe was too risky. But he needed to breathe. He opened his mouth and thought of a landed fish flapping on a wooden dock, mouth agape, trying to breathe.

The RV moved, then braked.

Spots flitted across his vision.

If he passed out, who knew how long before they would haul him out from his hiding place? He needed air. Now.

The RV moved.

He grabbed the duffel bag on his face and went to push it out but hesitated. What if a customs officer looks through the windshield, staring down the hallway? What if someone sees the bag move?

The RV edged forward.

He shoved the bag out and sucked in glorious air.

"Good morning," Daniel said from the front, his voice barely discernible from where Parkman lay.

"Passports?"

Silence followed. Then, "What is your purpose in Mexico?"

Parkman breathed in blessed air.

"Martial arts tournament and conference south of Tijuana. Also, sun and sand at the beaches."

"Yeah," Benjamin chimed in, his voice overly happy.

"How many in the vehicle, sir?"

"Just the three of us."

He'd warned him not to say *just*.

Parkman took one last long breath, held it, and eased the duffel bag back in place.

Then, in a gruff voice, loud enough for Parkman to hear from his hiding place, the officer said, "Pull the vehicle over there. Do it now. Then turn off the RV and remove the keys."

Parkman's heart skipped a beat. Pressure in his head pounded. Moisture in his mouth disappeared, leaving behind a dry, cotton-like mouth.

The RV moved.

Chapter 9

"This isn't going to work," Sarah said. "Vivian's remaining quiet. She won't give up cartel dealings for the DEA."

"Will she give them up for you?" Darwin asked.

"What do you mean?"

"Give us a detail, a drop location, a place where cartel members will meet, and we'll hit it instead of the DEA. We can add pressure to the cartel ourselves. Is that something that'll get her talking?"

Sarah shook her head. "She talks when she wants to."

"Then we're stuck. The Enzo Cartel is extremely secretive, and for a good reason. Two other cartels already own this territory; since Tijuana is a border town, this is prime land. Keeping to themselves, the newly formed Enzo Cartel avoids war with the others. For now. But that also means we can't find them without Vivian."

"They didn't keep to themselves when they took Aaron."

Darwin glanced at her sidelong. "But they didn't expect you to be a threat."

Sarah paced the cabin floor. She walked to the window and stared outside. Thoughts of Casper and what had happened to the authorities in that hotel filled her mind. He was probably dead like so many of them. She would be dead by now had Vivian not directed her to attend church.

All those agents were dead, and the newspapers weren't releasing names yet. Even when they did, Casper's name probably wouldn't appear in the news.

A phone rang. Darwin jumped for it.

"Who's that?" Sarah asked.

"Rosina. She's the only one with this number." He raised a hand as he pushed a series of buttons. "Don't worry. This satellite phone is encrypted." He brought it to his ear and stood beside her by the big front window.

"What have you found out?" he asked.

Darwin listened for a moment, keeping his eyes off Sarah. Then he lowered the phone and punched in a code. After a moment, he turned and placed the Sat phone on a corner table.

"Are you going to tell me?" Sarah asked.

"Rosina says hi."

"That's why she called?" Sarah put her hands on her hips. "There's more. Tell me."

"Because Parkman was taken, they've deduced there's been a leak. They're trying to plug it."

"What about my parents?" Sarah asked, hysteria settling in over her system. "They're in a safe house as well. How long before they're taken because of a *leak*? How fucking powerful is this cartel?"

"I'm sorry, Sarah." He came over to her. "I know how much Parkman meant to you."

"Don't. No, you don't. Do not speak about him as if he's dead. Until I see a body, Parkman is alive and well."

"You're right. I'm sorry."

Sarah plopped on the couch and dropped her face in her hands. "I can't believe this. It's like my world is falling apart." Despair clouded her thoughts. "They take Aaron. Attack the hotel. Casper's probably dead. And now they've got Parkman."

"They're moving your parents and have doubled their agent detail. That's all Rosina could get, but she'll keep us posted."

Sarah rubbed her face and then looked up at Darwin. "Now what?" she asked. "I've never felt so lost."

"We have no choice but to attack the cartel as soon as possible."

"But how? Vivian's gone. She's offering nothing. We don't know where the cartel is. We have nothing to go on."

He moved to the couch and sat beside her. "The problem is time. They're taking action against us every day while we sit here in seclusion. We have to do something, anything. If that means driving around Tijuana and looking for *falcones*, then that's what we do. We'll come loaded for war and search the streets until we're seen or see them. It's all I've got."

"Then let's do it, but I can't promise when we bump into them on the street that I'll keep any of them alive." She shook her head, hair flying up. "No, after what they've done, no one lives."

Darwin grabbed the guitar case full of guns and grenades and headed for the door.

"No one lives," he repeated and stepped outside.

Sarah followed him outside, asking Vivian to wake up and give her something to work with.

Before Sarah reached the Hummer, Vivian's presence oozed into her consciousness with a soft message.

I hate what becomes of you over the coming days, Vivian whispered. *I don't want to watch.*

"Why?" Sarah snapped. "Why can't you watch?"

Darwin spun around to stare at her.

Because I love you too much, baby sister.

"Tell me what's going to happen," Sarah demanded.

I'm going to lose you ...

Vivian's essence moved away. Sarah hopped inside the Hummer, chambered a round into her handgun, and looked over at Darwin.

"You coming? Let's go kill us a cartel."

Darwin walked around, got in the driver's seat, and started the Hummer.

With one last look at Sarah, he pulled away from the cabin.

Chapter 10

CASPER WAS SHOVED OFF the helicopter when it was still five feet from setting down on the helipad. The carpet of well-manicured grass offered a soft landing, but the impact still forced a grunt to escape his lips.

Before he could get to his feet, hands that felt like slabs of marble hoisted him up and dragged him toward the small prison cell he had once shared with Aaron.

The fight beat out of him, and the remorse he felt over the loss of Aaron was too much, so he allowed himself to be dragged all the way to the chained door.

Outside the door, waiting for it to be unlocked, the sun burned his back. He yearned for them to hurry, to let him in where he'd be out of the direct sun. But then what? What was next? More killings? Or would they torture him for answers he couldn't offer?

The door was finally unlocked. One of the men swung it

open while the other charged inside and dropped him in the middle of the cell.

The men retreated, slammed the door, and applied external locks.

"I thought you'd never come back," a man sounding like Aaron said.

Casper shot his head up. "Is that you? Aaron?"

"Who else would it be?"

"But you're dead!" Casper nearly shouted. "I saw you fall out of the helicopter."

"Yes, you did. But I'm not dead."

Casper got on his knees and crawled to Aaron, where he touched his face, blew out a long sigh, and then plopped down beside him.

"What happened?" Casper said.

"They planned it from the beginning."

"How? How did you know their plans?"

"Those two men were killed for some infraction unrelated to us and our situation. They did it in front of us to show you how serious they are. Then the pilot flew away from where those bodies were dumped and hovered over their water reservoir."

"Reservoir?" Casper glanced up at Aaron.

"When I jumped on the guy suspended from the safety line, I looked down. We were a high-diving board height away from a large rectangular reservoir. Spanish had two divers already in the water, waiting for my inevitable fall. The sun glinted off one of their face masks. I knew I'd be saved and brought back here when I hit the water."

Casper blew pent-up air out of his mouth. "I thought you died back there."

"That's what they wanted you to think."

"The reservoir's that big?"

Aaron nodded, then ran a hand through his hair. "It's at the back edge of the tree line."

Casper had a revelation. "I thought I saw the roof of the main house just before you leaped out of the chopper. We didn't have far to fly back after you were gone."

"They need me alive for Sarah. I have to be their last resort. But I'm no good to them after they catch her."

Casper faced Aaron. "You're that certain they're going to catch Sarah?"

Aaron nodded.

Casper clapped his hands together. "We have to get you out of here. Once Sarah sees you're safe, she'll back off because if the Enzo Cartel gets their hands on Sarah, they'll kill her before Vivian has anything to say about it. Vivian can't stop bullets."

"How do you propose I escape this place?" Aaron asked.

"You're good with your hands, right?"

"With my hand like this"—he held up the bandaged one that was missing a finger—"I only have one good hand."

"And your feet."

"True."

"I have a plan."

"Tell me."

Casper leaned in closer and explained his idea to Aaron.

"If everything goes just right, I could see that working," Aaron said.

"Then let's make sure everything goes just right."

After a minute, Casper witnessed one of the first genuine smiles on Aaron's face since arriving.

Casper knew he would be dead this time tomorrow because of the escape idea, but at least Aaron liked the plan. There was that.

Chapter 11

THE RV CAME TO a complete stop. The engine cut off. Parkman breathed slowly, listening for movement at the front of the vehicle. The boys' voices trailed off as they were led away from the RV.

As much as he didn't want to, Parkman had to move the duffel bag to access more air. He'd pass out if he didn't. Being discovered by the Mexican authorities wasn't a problem for him. He was a kidnap victim. They would parade him in front of the media, showing the Americans that Mexican customs officers were on the job.

The problem of discovery lay at Daniel, Benjamin, and Alex's doorstep. They would be charged with federal offenses as they snatched Parkman from an FBI safe house and tried to cross an international border with him. The three of them would be tied up in the court system long after the Sarah and Aaron issue was dealt with and would spend longer in prison.

But that was only if they discovered Parkman. No one knew Aaron's teachers had taken him. If the RV was empty, then all the Mexican authorities had were three Canadian martial arts boys on an impromptu trip to Mexico for a tournament. Nothing wrong with that. Denied entry or not, they'd done nothing wrong if the RV was empty.

Claiming to be a stowaway wouldn't work. Once all the details were ironed out, they would know that Parkman had been taken. But it wasn't against his will. He wanted to join the fight to save Aaron. He wanted to be in Mexico and not lingering in a safe house, watching TV and waiting on news of Sarah.

So what now? Hope he didn't get discovered or leave the RV.

He listened for telltale signs that someone was on board but heard nothing. A door opened and closed somewhere outside the RV. Sounds floated to him—traffic, a car engine backfired, someone laughed—but nothing seemed too close.

Could he simply get up and walk away from the RV? Maybe hitch a ride somewhere? Weren't they already on Mexican soil? Didn't Mexican laws pertain to this area?

Then someone stepped onto the RV. A loud bang resounded throughout the vehicle, and he jumped. Being hidden under the bed kept his movement undetectable.

The bathroom door opened. The drawers were rifled through. The door slammed. A closet was opened. The searcher spoke softly to himself. The tone was one of boredom and laziness. Something else banged.

Parkman hadn't pulled the duffel bag back in, but now it was too late. Moving the bag now could prove dangerous.

His nerves pinging, mouth wide open, eyes wide, and feeling frantic, Parkman slid his right hand down his side until it bumped his weapon. Slowly, as the customs officer examined the RV near the bedroom, Parkman pulled the weapon and brought it up to aim where he would look under the bed.

He waited.

More bangs. More shudders. The RV rocked slightly.

The duffel bag by Parkman's face was kicked. The customs officer stopped moving.

"Perfecto," he whispered.

The duffel bag was yanked out, exposing Parkman's face to bright sunshine.

The officer wasn't looking under the bed. He opened the bag and rifled through the clothes Daniel had brought along.

Parkman was grateful the officer hadn't pulled the other bag that held all their weapons. He moved the tip of the gun to aim at the officer's lower leg and waited for him to finish, wondering why he hadn't looked to his right yet.

The officer had to be twenty years old. His face glistened with sweat, and his hands shook. Why was he searching the RV alone?

Then it all became clear.

The customs officer produced a little baggie filled with white powder and dropped it inside the duffel bag. At that moment, Parkman understood everything. They were framing the three boys. But for what? The RV? What could Daniel, Benjamin, and Alex have that the Mexican authorities wanted to arrest them on drug charges at the border?

Unless they were made as Aaron's teachers. That Mexican student Aaron had, with alleged ties to the Enzo

Cartel, could have supplied pictures of the teachers. The cartel would have a few customs guards in their pockets. Or they simply had Mexican authorities supply the photos to customs to watch for them. However it came to be, Aaron's teachers were in a world of trouble and wouldn't see the outside of a Mexican prison for many years.

Unless Parkman could do something about it.

The young officer zipped the bag closed with the drugs on the inside and was about to shove the bag back when Parkman cocked the weapon.

The officer snapped his head toward Parkman, eyes wider than any Parkman had ever seen.

"Easy," he said. "Move, and I will blow a hole in your kneecap."

Chapter 12

SARAH RODE SHOTGUN, LITERALLY. A large gun rested between her legs as Darwin raced through the streets of Tijuana like American soldiers speeding through the streets of Baghdad in their Humvees. They passed hundreds of faces, some devious, some offering cold stares, but none appearing hostile. At no point did they pass any Mexican police.

"I'll head south of Tijuana," Darwin said. "Let's see what's down there."

"Good, because nothing's happening here. I'm getting antsy sitting around, watching the buildings pass by."

"Is there anything else we could be doing?" Darwin asked.

Sarah shrugged one shoulder. "I have no idea. We have no help from the authorities. Vivian's quiet. We're completely on our own, and we have no idea where the Enzo Cartel is keeping Aaron. Darwin, I think I'm losing my mind."

She tapped her foot and bit into a thumbnail, trying to hold back the tears.

Darwin turned onto the Via Rápida José Fimbres Moreno Highway and headed southbound. They rode in silence for five minutes before Darwin gripped the wheel with both hands.

"I think we're being followed," he said.

Sarah lowered in her seat and tried to locate the tail in the square Hummer mirror on her side. A black car stayed back about a hundred yards, pacing them.

"I see two men in the front," Sarah said.

"Agreed."

"Is that an Impala?"

"Looks like it."

"Feds?"

"Doubt it."

"Then leave the highway and lead them to a secluded area and let me out when they lose sight of us briefly. Drive twenty yards and turn off the engine. I'll do the rest."

Darwin turned her way. "You sure?"

"Never more sure. Do it. They could lead us to Aaron."

Darwin reduced the Hummer's speed and changed lanes to prepare to exit the highway.

Chapter 13

Diego studied the back of the Hummer like it would magically disappear if he looked away.

"We're going to be rich, man," Diego said. "I can see it now."

Mateo drove well, even with a few beers in him. It was Mateo's car, so Mateo drove, but Diego had tried to persuade him at the bar that maybe he should drive since he hadn't drunk anything. But no, it was Mateo's car.

Diego didn't believe it when they first saw the Hummer that Enzo's people said needed to be located. Like a gift, it pulled onto the highway right in front of them. Merged into traffic, pulled in front, and drove along like a lure to a waiting fish. The difference was this fish was a shark, and the lure was easy prey. Mateo had immediately called in to his contact and was ordered to tail the Hummer until Enzo's people could get in place.

Diego slapped the dash above the glove box. "Damn, won't those Enzo people make us rich now?"

"Hey," Mateo yelled. "Watch the fucking car. Don't slap my shit."

"Take it easy, Homey." Diego took his eyes off the Hummer for the time it took to look at Mateo. "When this is over, I'll buy you a new car with the hundreds of thousands Enzo has put down for this stupid *chocho*."

Mateo's face had broken out in a glistening sweat.

"What's wrong, *cuate*?" Diego asked as he turned back to watch the Hummer. "Scared to get your hands dirty?"

"I gotta piss, man. Something fierce."

"You drank two beers. C'mon, you can hold it." He playfully punched Mateo in the arm. "There's no letting this Hummer out of our sight."

"Don't fucking touch me."

"Hey, take it easy. Just playing around."

"Just don't touch me, or I'll pull this car over and do some real hurting."

"Lose the tough act, Ese, and follow the Hummer. This ain't no time to be fighting."

Diego rubbed his thighs and watched as the Hummer changed lanes. "Follow them, man."

"What do you think I'm doing?"

The Hummer exited the highway at Boulevard Manuel J. Clothier and turned onto a residential street in the Castro Green area.

"You know this area?" Diego asked.

"Yeah, my cousin lived two blocks from here before going into the joint. I got this."

The Hummer turned a corner and disappeared for a

moment. When they reacquired the target, it sped up. Mateo called in the new location and dropped his phone between his legs.

"You think they made us?" Diego asked, starting to sweat a little.

"I got this, I said," Mateo shouted. "I know how to follow people."

"Didn't say that, shit for brains. Just asking is all."

"Call me that again," Mateo shouted.

"Take it easy," Diego pleaded. "This is easy money. You want me to call that Enzo guy I know? Tell him where the Hummer is?"

"No. I called it in twice. You stay off the phone. We'll deal with this. If they stop anywhere, we'll knock the fuckers out, and I'll drive the Hummer to the Enzo Cartel, gift-wrapped with its captives inside."

"Who's gonna drive your Impala?" Diego asked, always wanting to drive the Impala, hoping to get that chance.

"You, dumbass. But if you fuck it up, you pay for it twice out of your forty percent."

"Twice! No way—" he stopped talking. Then, "Hey, wait a sec. What forty percent? I saw the Hummer first. Fifty-fifty or fuck off."

"Ain't no fifty-fifty," Mateo growled. "It's my car we followed them in. I'm gettin' reimbursed for that shit."

"Ain't no money for nobody if you don't focus on the job," Diego said, pointing out the windshield. "They're getting away."

The Hummer had turned another corner up ahead where the street narrowed and was lost to sight again. It would take Mateo a precious five seconds or more to get to the corner.

He revved the engine as the Impala shot forward. He came around too fast at the corner, the back tires emitting a minor squeal.

The Hummer had stopped by a grassy patch.

Mateo jammed the brakes, slowed to a crawl, then stopped twenty yards behind Hummer.

"What now?" Diego asked. He wiped the sweat out of his eyes. "Can't you turn up this air conditioning shit?"

He switched a dial on the dash. Mateo slapped his hand away.

"Don't fucking touch the car. You're only allowed to sit in it, *pendejo*."

"Fuck you," Diego said. "I need air, then." He rolled his window down.

A cold piece of metal jammed against his cheek so far his head was pushed sideways, almost landing on Mateo's shoulder.

"Turn the car off or paint the interior red," a girl said. "I don't really care which."

The gun pressed painfully into his skin. His vision was tilted sideways, but he could still see a man hop out of the Hummer with a gun in each hand.

In public, Diego shouted inside his head.

Mateo reached up slowly and turned off the car.

"Pull the keys and toss them out your window."

Mateo obeyed.

"Hands on the steering wheel," the girl ordered. "You," she poked Diego's cheek harder. "Hands on the dash."

The man with a gun in each hand opened Mateo's door and yanked him out so hard Mateo sprawled out on the concrete. Then the guy kicked Mateo in the gut.

The girl eased off.

"Out of the car."

Diego hesitated. He had no play. His gun was beside him, but she would press her trigger the moment he took his hands off the dash to go for it.

From the corner of his eye, the man was yanking Mateo to his feet. Tough Mateo. Stupid Mateo. Silent now that he'd been one-upped.

But Diego wouldn't be one-upped. No *bruja* was going to get the drop on him. Once he took her out, he'd hide behind the car until he shot the guy with the two guns. After piling their bodies in the back of the Hummer, he'd deliver them to the Enzo people and collect his cash. All one hundred percent of it.

Shit, man, fucking idiots just made things easy.

"Okay, don't shoot," Diego said. "I'm going to take my hands off the dash as I turn to get out."

"Slowly," the girl said, her voice steady as a rock.

She'd done this before. He saw it in her eyes. This was one tough bitch. But not tougher than a bullet.

Fuck you.

He eased to the right to get out and lowered his hands. His left hand dropped to the seat as if to push off, then darted behind him, grabbed the butt of the weapon, and the gun went off.

The girl punched him hard in the chest, and his breathing instantly grew difficult. So difficult that he slumped in the seat, unable to breathe like he got the wind knocked out of him.

In a moment of clarity, he realized his gun hadn't fired. The girl saw what he was about to do and shot him. The punch in the chest was her bullet. The difficulty in breathing was a punctured lung.

He was dying because a stupid *bruja* got the jump on him. What would his mother think?

Stupid bruja.

In a crazy effort to live, he sucked air in through a wheezy tube. But it wasn't enough. Liquid pooled in his crotch. Spots formed in his vision. The pain hadn't really set in yet. It was more of a pressure issue. Discomfort. But the pain would come, he was sure of it. Unbearable pain. He would need a hospital. Morphine. Lots of drugs.

He wanted to see the girl one more time. The effort was as great as climbing a mountain road after an ironman triathlon. He forced his head up and looked at the complacent face of the blonde bitch that shot him. How could she? They didn't know each other. And now it was over. The end.

As if his head was leaden down with rocks, it dropped, and his chin bounced once off his chest as he slumped sideways in Mateo's seat.

Mateo's going to be pissed about the car.

What little air was left in his lung seemed to leave through the hole in his chest.

Chapter 14

SARAH SHRUGGED AND RAISED her hands.

"He went for his gun."

"Kill them all," Darwin said. "I'm happier that way, Sarah. But we need information. Kill them after we learn shit. Cool?"

Sarah nodded and approached the Impala's hood to meet the driver.

"Sorry about that."

"Better."

She bent down to the driver. "What's your name?" she asked in a friendly manner. The same tone she would use if they were buying popcorn at the local movie theater before a movie.

"Mateo."

"Okay, Mateo. Why were you following us?"

"Nice wheels. Thought about jacking it."

"Bullshit." Sarah smiled and scanned the neighborhood. All the houses in close proximity seemed quiet behind their gated driveways and lawns. Curiosity had not pulled anyone outside yet. But people would come soon. The authorities were probably already on their way.

She chambered a round and made her weapon the third gun aimed at Mateo.

"Why did you follow us? Making me ask twice pisses me off. A third time ends your life."

A dark spot formed on Mateo's jeans about the crotch and spread. It leaked out onto the pavement below his ass.

"He pissed himself," Darwin stated in a bland tone. He genuinely seemed bored.

How this looked to Mateo would probably scare the shit out of him, but Sarah was done with the *hope*. *Hoping* to find Aaron. *Hoping* Aaron was still alive. *Hoping* the authorities would do the right thing. There would be no more *hoping*.

She placed the gun against the top of Mateo's head.

"Gonna tell me?" Sarah asked. "Or die in the street like a fucking pig?"

Most men, when faced with this prospect, especially after witnessing her execute his friend moments before, would spill the beans on their own mother. And Mateo didn't disappoint.

He rambled on about the Enzo Cartel and the bounty on the Hummer. The alive-or-dead caveat and how there were hundreds of soldiers looking for that Hummer and its occupants.

As he fumbled over his words, cried, and shook with panic, Sarah eased the gun off his skull and stepped back. Darwin lowered his guns, aiming them at the pavement.

"Looks like the cartel is going to come to us after all," Darwin said.

Mateo frowned. "You guys want the cartel after you?"

Sarah nodded. "I'm here to put an end to the Enzo Cartel. But I don't take prisoners."

"Why's that?" Mateo asked.

"No one lives."

Darwin shot Mateo in each foot simultaneously and started away.

"Darwin, I thought we had a deal. No one lives."

Darwin called over his shoulder. "No cartel members get a pass. He's not cartel."

Mateo screamed and writhed on the pavement.

"Almost as much," Sarah called after him. "He was working for them."

"He can't hurt us again. By the time that heals and he's walking with canes—if he can ever walk again—this'll be long over. Come on. Jump in. We got business."

Sarah turned to Mateo. "You might want to put a tourniquet on that, or you'll bleed to death. Use your friend's belt or shirt or something." She stepped away, slipping her gun into her waistband. "Gotta run. Remember, no one lives. You got lucky."

Sarah ran over and jumped in the Hummer.

"Didn't we scare the shit out of him?" Sarah said.

Darwin checked his mirrors and got the Hummer rolling. "I thought you were going to kill him back there."

"I'm not killing anybody unless they deserve it. When his friend went for the gun, I reacted. He died. It happens. But I wanted Mateo to think I would kill him, and I accomplished that."

"All we accomplished was exposure. Just like last night. The cartel works fast. They're all searching for this beast. What do you think about getting off the road, finding another vehicle?"

"No way," Sarah said as she sat back in the passenger seat. "We stay in the Hummer. We wait for them to come to us. Then we nail them and say, 'Take us to your leader.'"

"Jokes at a time like this?" Darwin asked as he signaled and turned a corner.

"Is there a better time to—"

A dump truck came out of nowhere and slammed into the passenger side of the Hummer, shoving Sarah sideways and showering her with glass.

Chapter 15

"ARE YOU SMART, OR are you stupid?" Parkman asked.

His shoulder was beginning to ache in the twisted position he had taken under the bed. His arms were extended, and the gun was aimed at the Mexican customs officer at an angle.

The young man blinked once and continued to stare at Parkman.

"You see," Parkman continued, "smart men do smart things, and stupid men do stupid things. What I just saw you do was stupid. But you could still play this smart. If you get up and try to run from this RV, that would be stupid. Before you got to the door, I'd cut you in half with this hand cannon. You see how stupid that would be?"

The officer nodded.

"Good. So get on that radio on your belt and tell them the RV is clean. Your search is over. But you're leaving the drugs. Got it."

Parkman's gun hand didn't waver. But it did move to aim at the man's right cheek.

"Radio it in," Parkman said, his voice firmer. "You're out of options. My little friend here has limited your decision process to doing what I say. So, do as I say. Do it now."

The guard moved slowly, unclipped his radio, depressed the button, and called in the all-clear, keeping his eyes on Parkman's face the whole time.

"Good. Now, slide that radio to me."

The officer set it down and tried to slide it, but it rolled on the thinly carpeted floor of the RV.

"Where's your gun?"

This was risky and a time waster. They needed to leave the area as fast as possible now that he had drawn on a customs officer. But how? Parkman couldn't let this officer just walk out of the RV. They wouldn't get two miles before they were apprehended.

Kidnap him?

The real question was how far they were willing to go; how many laws were they willing to break before too much was too much? Find Aaron, save him, but spend ten years in prison for doing it?

Parkman knew he had reached the point of no return when he allowed Aaron's teachers to convince him to come along.

"Cross the border into Mexico. It'll be fine. We have a story," they said. "Nothing bad will happen."

But now something had happened. And this officer was going to bust them on possession of cocaine after planting it.

Would Sarah let that slide?

Maybe he hadn't been around her enough recently. Perhaps he was getting soft.

Well, not anymore.

"Turn around and place your back to the wall. Do it now."

To his delight, the guard did exactly as he was told.

"Sit on your hands."

The officer eased them under his buttocks.

"Good. See, you're smart, after all."

Voices approached from outside the RV. Someone shouted for José.

"Is that you?" Parkman whispered. "Are you José?"

The officer nodded slowly.

"Shout back that you're just finishing, and you'll be out in a minute."

José complied.

The man outside slapped the side of the RV.

"Okay, but hurry up. We've got another one to search."

The RV shook as someone entered it. Parkman detected multiple voices.

Then he heard Aaron's teachers. The moment Parkman was certain it was them, they stopped talking. The RV stopped moving.

"It's okay, boys," Parkman whispered loud enough to be heard. "He's with us."

Someone walked the length of the RV and stopped in front of the officer. Parkman recognized the thin shins and knew it was Alex.

"We're cool, Alex. Just get Daniel to drive us the fuck out of here. Do it now. This guy won't give us any trouble."

The RV's engine fired up. Then it was moving. Moments

later, it was doing highway speed.

"Why are we kidnapping a Mexican border guard?" Benjamin asked.

"He dropped a bag of cocaine in that duffel bag. He tried to frame you boys, and I want to know why."

"Me too," Alex stated in his quiet but menacing voice. "Me too."

Then he made some super-fast move that Parkman only saw as a blur, and the officer's head dropped, and his body slumped.

"What did you do?" Parkman asked as he pushed his way out from under the bed.

"Put him to sleep. He'll be up in ten minutes or so."

"Okay," Parkman rubbed his legs where they had gone to sleep under the bed. "But we need to talk about how we treat the people we kidnap."

"How about we talk about not kidnapping people?" Benjamin said.

"Point taken, but I couldn't let him leave the RV and report us. We wouldn't make it five miles."

"Point taken," Alex mimicked. "They're going to notice he's gone, though. Then come after us."

Parkman looked out the back window. "True. We need to change vehicles."

"How?" Daniel shouted from the front. "Where?"

"No idea. But get off the highway. I'll think of something."

Daniel hit his indicator and exited the highway. There had been an accident up ahead. It looked like a dump truck had T-boned a Hummer. No emergency vehicles were close by, and there were no sirens to be heard.

"That just happened," Parkman said. "Steer around it. Get us out of here. The authorities are probably responding now, and we don't want to be here when they do."

Daniel slowed and expertly steered around the front of the Hummer, then shot the RV forward. The workers in the dump truck were just getting out of their vehicle when Parkman pulled a curtain back and looked back at the accident.

For a brief moment, Parkman caught a glimpse inside the windshield of the Hummer and thought he saw Sarah in the passenger seat, her head resting on her left shoulder.

If he was mistaken and it wasn't Sarah, then the girl in the Hummer was Sarah's doppelgänger.

He almost made Daniel turn back.

Chapter 16

Food was delivered, the door locked, and the sunlight blocked, but the heat and the humidity remained. Even though his stomach begged for a bite, Casper gave up his portion to strengthen Aaron.

"Casper, you need to eat," Aaron said. "You'll wither away, lose what strength you have, and be useless to anyone."

"You're escaping tonight. If I live through the night, I'll eat tomorrow."

"How are you so sure this plan will work?" Aaron asked between bites of refried beans and bread.

"If they wanted you dead, they would have killed you. This is a no-brainer. They can't afford to have you die yet. If they think I'm going to kill you, they will come in here and stop me."

"And the rest is history," Aaron ended.

"We have to author our own destiny. If you're meant to have a destiny past this night, then you have to leave this place. Once you're out, Sarah can leave Mexico with you." Casper rolled over and faced him. "How are you feeling? Your fatigue leaving, strength coming back?"

"Much better." Aaron lowered his head.

"What?" Casper asked. "What is it?" He pulled himself up to sit cross-legged. "What's bothering you?"

Aaron wiped his eyes. "I don't know what happened to me."

"How do you mean?"

"They snatched me, brought me here, and I crumbled." He sniffled and wiped his nose. "The waterboarding, the thought of dying. Then poor Hector was killed in front of me, and his corpse was left in here overnight."

"They were trying to break you. To them, this is a game. They break you to get what they want. Once they have Sarah, you're both discarded like an unwanted child's toy. I'm sorry, but that's the reality of it."

Aaron met Casper's gaze. "Unless I do something about it?"

Casper nodded.

"I could be killed tonight," Aaron added.

Casper nodded. "The odds will increase with what we're proposing."

"But I'll be killed regardless, so what's the difference?"

"Maybe there's something to what Sarah does. I mean, aren't we describing her philosophy? Don't wait for the threat to be met; run up to it. Deal with it and be done with it. Waiting will only get you killed."

"Yeah," Aaron said, emotion constricting his vocal cords.

"If it were Sarah, she'd do it with one hand tied behind her back. That's literally how I'm going to have to do it as this hand," he held up his bandaged right, "is useless to me."

"Tonight, Aaron. As planned. Tonight you win your freedom. Not long now." Casper lay back and closed his eyes. "As soon as the sun goes down."

They sat in silence for some time. Casper's mind began to wander, about to be lost in dreams, as he floated back to sleep.

"Casper?" Aaron said.

Startled, Casper jerked awake. "Yeah?"

"When we do this, I aim to kill Spanish."

Casper rested back in position, hoping his heart rate would calm so he could sleep.

"I expect you to, Aaron. Spanish needs to die. I would think nothing less of you. You're the man who's with Sarah Roberts." He breathed in a couple of times, eyes closed. "Nothing less," he whispered, then nodded off.

Chapter 17

SARAH GASPED AS THE Hummer settled. She remained completely still to do a mental inventory of her body.

What the hell just happened?

The dump truck. The accident. Shattered glass covered her, and the armrest jammed painfully into her ribcage.

She took a deep breath and winced. A rib was cracked or broken. Maybe more than one. The pain increased in waves with each breath.

Shit! I can't have this now.

She slid a foot sideways until it found the shotgun she had been cradling. She needed the gun in her hands. She needed it ready. She had to bend forward to retrieve it. But the pain in her ribs stopped her.

An RV slowed, drove around them, then accelerated away. She watched it retreat. Someone at the rear of the RV pulled a curtain back and looked at her. A man. Then the RV turned a corner and disappeared.

The dump truck's doors closed. Whoever hit them had gotten out with no regard for the noise they made.

Darwin moaned beside her.

She needed that gun.

Be kidnapped. Be killed in the street. Be tortured. Or … reach down and get that gun.

But the pain in her ribs grew with each passing moment.

Fuck it!

Sarah let out a primal scream as she lunged forward, wrapped her hand around the barrel of the shotgun, and sat back up, pumping a round into ready.

The pain sliced through her like the edge of a dull saw blade caressing her ribs. Her vision clouded with the pressure. It felt like the pain was all she could focus on for the moment.

But the gun was in her hands, and the lethal end was aimed out the broken window beside her. The rearview mirror was pulverized. The dump truck's grill filled most of her vision, but because the Hummer rode so high, she saw into the cab of the empty dump truck. No one was in sight. It had been a full minute. Where were the sirens? Darwin stirred beside her again.

"Hey!" she said. "Wake up."

Darwin moaned. He touched the side of his neck.

"Darwin. We have company somewhere. You need to be present. Wake up."

His eyes opened.

"Get a gun in your hand," she whispered urgently, the pain keeping her mouth tight.

Darwin was a fighter, but the accident seemed to have

knocked something loose. He was slowly reaching for his weapon.

Her damaged door was no longer an exit. She would have to crawl across the large center console and leave through Darwin's door, which was not an inviting thought.

I'll need morphine to make it out of this vehicle.

An acrid smell rose from under the Hummer. Something leaked from the accident. Maybe something was burning.

Darwin seemed to be awake now, but his eyes were glazed. He looked like he'd been awakened from a dead sleep and wasn't sure where he was yet.

"Darwin," Sarah said in an even voice, her breaths coming in short, sharp waves. "Please wake the fuck up and look around. We have two possible enemies outside the Hummer. I can't see shit with this dump truck up my ass." Darwin looked at her, his deadpan expression offering nothing coherent. "You think you could get on board with this idea and kill those bastards that did this?"

The acrid smell intensified. Something definitely was burning.

"Darwin, smell that?"

He sniffed the air. "Shit, Sarah, what happened?"

"You're going to die, Darwin," she snapped through gritted teeth.

"I am?" It was as if he was ten years old again, and his mother just said he was about to be punished.

"If you don't pull it together and deal with this, I *will* kill you."

He stared at her for a prolonged period. The burning smell filled the cab now.

Sarah raised the butt of the shotgun, scrunched her face

at the pain, and jabbed Darwin's shoulder.

"Hey!" she shouted.

After being shoved into the corner and bouncing back, he blinked several times, then his face creased into a frown.

"Why'd you do that?" he asked.

"There you are." She inhaled slowly. "You're back."

The dead stare had disappeared. Just in time because now she heard the familiar lick of a flame.

"The Hummer is on fire," Sarah said. "We need to leave. Now."

"Where's the asshole who drove into us?" Darwin asked. He had a gun in each hand now.

"There were two men in the dump truck."

Darwin looked outside his window.

The high-pitched ping of a ricochet bounced off the hood of the Hummer as Darwin jerked his head back.

"They've got us pinned down," he said.

A flame lifted from under the hood on the passenger side.

"We're going to cook in here. How long before you think this thing will blow?"

"No idea. Any second."

"Gee. You're helpful." She took a breath in. "That doesn't. Inspire hope."

"Not here to inspire hope. I'm here to live."

"Then shoot. Those bastards." Another measured breath. "And let's get." A breath. "Out of here."

Darwin searched her face. "Why are you talking like that?"

"Ribs." She breathed through her clenched teeth and pursed lips. "Cracked bad or broken."

"And you picked up that shotgun?"

"Better the pain," she stopped to breathe, "than death."

"Okay. You got me there. One nothing for you."

"This isn't hockey."

"Everything is about scoring."

"Okay." She faced him. "Then beat them. Kill them. Whatever." She breathed. "But get me to a hospital. And let's stop talking," she clenched her jaw and breathed, "in a Hummer that's about to explode."

"Right. Got it."

Darwin extended his hands out the window and began firing toward the shooter. The flames rose higher.

There was a surprisingly strong response to Darwin's barrage. He had to lean close to Sarah to avoid getting hit by a ricochet.

While bent inward, he turned the key in the ignition. For some blessed reason, the stalled Hummer started up.

"Shit, that's crazy," Darwin said. Two more bullets dinged off the hood. Darwin and Sarah jolted in harmony. "Didn't think it would start."

He dropped it in four-wheel drive, waited for the light to indicate it was locked in, then hit the gas. The Hummer's engine ground like it was running coffee beans through it. The fire intensified, shooting flames out sideways. But it edged forward even though it was attached to the dump truck.

"This baby can hold a ton in the cargo and pull several tons on a trailer," Darwin shouted over the grinding engine.

"I'm glad you're," Sarah breathed in, "so happy about it."

The Hummer wasn't going straight. With the dump truck hooked to the side, the Hummer was forced to the right on a wide arc.

That sheltered Darwin to be able to get out of the Hummer.

He must've, too, as she thought of it, because he hit the trailer button on the dash telling the Hummer it was pulling something heavy, and dropped the accelerator. The Hummer performed a wide arc to the right until something metallic banged in the engine, and it stopped with a backfired protest. Flames rose from under the hood like someone was stoking a bonfire.

"We have to get out of this—" Sarah shouted but stopped as Darwin opened his door and dropped to the pavement.

Gunfire rattled outside; then Darwin returned fire.

He was on his own. She wanted to help, but crawling over the center console would be hell.

Yet she couldn't leave him out there on his own. The heat from the Hummer's fire reached through her broken window, burning her skin. In a few moments, her eyebrows would singe.

With the shotgun as a crutch, she pushed off the floor and tried to twist in her seat. The pain forced a white-hot sheet of cool sweat onto her skin. She felt the color drain from her face. A weapon fired twice outside.

Where are the police? What about neighbors? Isn't anyone going to call this in?

"This sucks," she said out loud. "What about Aaron, eh Vivian? Now what? I'm not of much use to anyone now."

More gunfire outside. The flames were inside the broken window now. If she were to sit up straight, her hair would catch fire.

Anger fueled her. Being trapped in a burning vehicle

while Darwin was under fire created a fury inside her that diminished the pain. It was the kind of anger that absolved her knuckles of torment during a fight. A paper cut stung when relaxed at home. But cut and bleeding knuckles during a rage-fueled fight didn't hurt at all. At least not until hours later when the rage was gone.

That rage built now. Being hindered by the pain in her ribs added to her helplessness, and if there was anything Sarah hated, it was helplessness.

She pushed off the seat with the shotgun, crawled over the center console, groaned deep as she raised her legs over the gear shift, and dropped into the driver's seat, panting with pain.

"Okay, that hurt more than I thought it would. Please don't pass out, please don't pass out."

Not one to pause too long, she hauled the shotgun up, checked it was ready to fire, and stuck her head around the corner.

Darwin was nowhere to be seen.

The top rim of a shooter's head protruded from behind an old Datsun. He brought his gun up, and just as she heard the weapon discharge, she pulled her head back.

The fire on the passenger side had grown, melting the plastic rim of the door and some of the inside roof. She had to get out, but the shooter had her pinned down.

"Okay, I give up," she shouted. "Come and get me."

"No way," a man shouted back. "I wait until you burn."

Shit, that didn't work.

"I'm going to jump out before I burn." The shouting was almost as painful as moving.

"I kill you if you come out."

She looked around the front of the Hummer, opened the center console, and rummaged inside. She pulled Darwin's Sat phone out and clipped it to her pocket. Rosina would need an update when they got out of this.

Something red caught her eye. She leaned back farther, wincing with the effort, and looked at a small fire extinguisher. It was too small to put the fire out under the hood, but it could have better uses.

She unclipped it and turned back to the open door. The man was still there, huddled behind the Datsun.

"See if this burns as hot when it explodes," she yelled, then tossed the red extinguisher at the Datsun with great effort, a yelp escaping her lips at the sharp pain in her ribs.

It landed far too early but rolled closer. It stopped ten feet from the Datsun. The man peered through the Datsun's windows at it, no doubt waiting for it to explode.

Sarah swung the shotgun around, aimed at the red canister, and fired.

She missed.

She pumped the weapon and fired again.

Missed again.

The man moved to the back of the Datsun. She pulled back inside the burning Hummer, the heat on her back severe. It could blow any time. She needed to leave.

Then the man stepped out from behind the Datsun and fired twice at the driver's side of the Hummer. When he stopped, Sarah leaned down sideways—ignoring the pain— to watch him stop at the fire extinguisher and pick it up. When he turned to run the ten feet to get behind the Datsun, Sarah rolled out of the Hummer, landed on her feet on the road—her right knee threatening to give out with the pain—

pumped the shotgun, aimed carefully with one second to go, and fired.

The front tire of the Datsun blew out. Chunks of metal bent inward on the front quarter panel. The rest of the damage was in the man's hamstring and upper calf. Before he dropped to his knees, his back still exposed to her, she had already pumped the weapon and was squeezing the trigger.

This time she hit him square in the back. The shooter dropped to his knees. He released the extinguisher. It fell beside him and rolled under the Datsun.

Sarah leaned against the Hummer and scanned around her, letting the shotgun tip lead the way, waiting for another shooter to appear, but none did.

The man she shot fell face forward and didn't move again. After a moment, Sarah tossed the shotgun back inside the Hummer, pulled the gun from her waistband, and started forward.

"Darwin?" she shouted and winced. "Darwin?"

The heat from the fire consuming the Hummer and the relentless sun made her seek shade. She moved down the street, passed two parked vehicles, and took cover behind an old GMC SUV.

Sirens roared in the distance.

Finally ...

A fast scan of the house to her right caught a curtain falling back into place. People were watching but staying out of the streets. Someone had called emergency services, and only now were they coming. An easy ten-minute delay.

A loud boom from the Hummer startled her. The hood blew open, and the fire raged from the center of it.

"Over here," a man shouted.

Sarah ducked low and moved around the SUV toward the sound.

Beside a white gate near a driveway to a residence, Darwin lay sprawled on the pavement.

"Here," he called to her.

"Any more shooters?" she asked before leaving cover.

"Only one."

"I got him."

"Then no."

She started toward Darwin cautiously. As she neared his position, she spotted another shooter lying face down beside Darwin.

"I got this guy just as he shot me in the arm. I couldn't use this hand so well to get the other guy by the Datsun. I have no aim with my left hand." He winced. "Sorry about that."

Sarah knelt slowly—scrunching up her face at the pain in her ribs—to look at Darwin's wound. "How bad is it?" she asked.

"Mostly a skin graze, but it numbed my arm something fierce."

"Must've hit a nerve." Sarah looked over her shoulder as emergency vehicles turned onto their street. "We have to toss the guns."

"Here, take them to the Hummer. Let them burn. I have more. Then I have to leave. They can't find me here." He got up on one elbow. "This is such a good thing. I can't believe how well this turned out."

"What?" Sarah collected the guns and got to her feet as a fire truck came to a stop on the other side of the Hummer. She looked down at Darwin and raised her eyebrows.

"You're kidding, right?"

"As I lie here thinking about it, this is great news."

"How's that?"

An ambulance pulled up behind the fire truck. Two police cars arrived behind it.

"You'll be taken to the hospital now. It's public. You'll be registered under your own name."

"And?"

"I'll go get patched on my own and head to the cabin, where I'll get my GPS tracker and weapons and come back to arm you at the hospital. As we discussed earlier, I think the cartel will come to the hospital within twelve hours of you being admitted to try to kill or kidnap you." He smiled wider. "They may come earlier than twelve hours. Then we'll have them."

"I'm glad to see you're so happy about that," Sarah said as she kicked his foot. "Can you smell my sarcasm?"

"They'll play right into our hands," he said, ignoring her question. "And take you to where they're holding Aaron. I'll monitor it on GPS and come get you. This could be all over this time tomorrow."

A paramedic headed their way.

"Gotta run, Sarah. See you at the hospital." He winked as he got up on his knees and ran bent over for the cover of a fence on the next property line.

She didn't wink back. Nor did she share in his enthusiasm. She headed for the Hummer, away from the paramedic. As the fire hose hit the windshield of the burning Hummer, Sarah tossed the weapons inside the open driver's side door and kept walking until she got to the ambulance.

"These guys attacked me and tried to steal my Hummer,"

she said. "Naturally, I defended myself."

A police officer walked up and pushed the paramedic aside.

"You have a lot of explaining to do, lady."

Sarah smiled, even though her ribs hurt like a bitch.

Chapter 18

Parkman moved to the front of the RV.

"Daniel, pull off the highway. We've been out here too long."

Daniel checked his mirrors and started to the right.

"What are you thinking, Parkman?" he asked.

"We need to change vehicles. They're going to miss the customs officer we have in the back and learn soon enough that this was the last vehicle he was sent to search. Then every cop within a fifty-mile radius will be looking for this vehicle."

"How do we get a new vehicle? We don't have the money to buy one."

Parkman stayed quiet while watching Daniel maneuver the RV off the highway. After several minutes, he turned toward the back.

"Where am I going?" Daniel asked.

"Pull over in a large parking lot somewhere. I need five minutes."

"Got it."

At the back, he bent down to face the officer who was still out.

"We need him awake," he said.

"We do?" Alex asked.

Parkman nodded. "He's our answer to changing vehicles."

"He is?"

Parkman shot Alex a pensive look. "Alex?"

"Yeah?"

"Can you wake him?"

Alex got down and slapped the officer twice. The man stirred, moaned.

"C'mon, wake up," Alex said. "Time to get up."

Parkman glanced at Benjamin, who sat watching from the corner of the bed. He shrugged and raised his eyebrows.

The RV took a hard right, pushing them all sideways.

The sound of smacking flesh was much louder this time as Alex laid into the officer.

To Parkman's surprise, the customs officer snapped awake and pressed his body into the carpet away from Alex.

"I have to warn you," Parkman said. "These men are quite capable of ending your life for what you did."

The RV turned one more corner, then slowed and came to a full stop.

"Parked," Daniel shouted from the front.

The officer looked from Alex to Parkman, then back to Alex. Parkman read the fear in the officer's eyes. He was told to do a job and fucked that up. The people who ordered him to leave drugs on the RV don't like fuckups. He's already in a world of trouble. If Parkman could make him fear them more, he'd get what he wanted.

"When you willingly entered this RV to plant narcotics, you pissed these boys off." Parkman glanced at Alex, then Benjamin. Daniel walked up behind him. "And when you piss these boys off, they exact a price for that. The last guy died in a fiery car accident."

"That's true, actually," Benjamin added as he got up off the bed. "In Greece."

"Let me talk to him," Parkman said softly.

Benjamin nodded.

Parkman addressed the officer. "These men are willing to let you live, though."

Hope filled the man's face. He blinked and swallowed the saliva he'd been holding.

"But you have to do something for us now."

"What?" the officer spoke the word with a tentative warble.

"We need to borrow your car."

Hope died in his face.

Parkman tightened his lips. "You do have a car, don't you?"

The man nodded. "It's at work."

Parkman slapped a fist into his other palm. "Shit. We're not going back to the border in this."

"We're not going back to the border at all," Daniel said. "Too dangerous."

Parkman sat on the bed in front of the young officer. "Tell us about your family. You live at home? Brothers? Sisters?"

"My mother. Live with her. One brother. Dead now."

The boys looked at each other.

"Sorry to hear that," Parkman said.

"Cartel business."

"Cartel?"

"They used him. Then he got dead."

"Tell me more," Parkman prodded.

"No money for us when growing up. I went school. Learn for this job at border. My brother went to street. Before my brother die, he say to me I have to meet his *cuate*. I was told I would be needed in future. That was it."

"How did your brother die?" Parkman asked.

"Someone call him a *soplón*."

"What's that?"

"A snitch." The officer rubbed his eyes and then looked back at Parkman. "He was flayed and skinned, then left to bleed out and die. Then, even before the funeral, they say to me I have his debt to pay. I been paying it ever since."

Parkman thought of another important question. "What cartel?"

"Enzo."

Alex clapped his hands together, making everyone jump simultaneously.

"Damn," Parkman said, looking at Alex. "Thanks for that."

Alex looked away, but he kept smiling.

"Do you know why we're here?" Parkman asked. "Did the people who told you to leave the narcotics also tell you why?"

He shook his head.

"We're in Mexico to shut down the Enzo Cartel."

The customs officer didn't appear to hear him at first. His expression remained unchanged. Then, slowly, his face filled with color, and tears dripped past his eyelids.

"You want me help?" he asked.

Parkman nodded slowly.

"What can I do?"

"We need a car. But not yours. Someone else's. Your mother's?"

He shook his head back and forth. "No car."

"Shit."

Parkman was stumped. He had ample cash in his account to buy a car but didn't want to use his bank accounts. It would alert the authorities to where he was, and he didn't want them going after Aaron's teachers.

"We still in Tijuana?" the customs officer asked.

"I pulled over on a road called Los Insurgentes," Daniel said. "We're parked on the side." He glanced outside. "Just down from a bank of some kind."

"That's good." The customs officer made to right himself and sit up, but Alex stepped in and set a foot on the man's leg, holding him down.

"I think it's okay for now," Parkman said. "Let's hear what he has to say first. He's unarmed, and he isn't going anywhere."

Alex lifted his foot off and moved away but remained very close, his body at the ready.

The young officer got up and put his back to the RV wall, the rear window above his head.

"I can get you a truck. An SUV. BMW."

"Yeah?" Parkman said. "How?"

"The man who gave me the drugs for you. He lives three

blocks from here. He works for Enzo. Small jobs. Here. There."

They all exchanged glances. This was better than Parkman could have hoped for. Maybe this new guy could lead them to where Aaron was being held.

"What's your name?" Parkman asked.

"Raúl, not José." He lowered his head. "Sorry about that. Back at the border, when that guy shouted for José to hurry up, I just thought, you know …"

Parkman shrugged. "Doesn't matter. Nice to meet you, Raúl." They shook hands. "It's time to get your revenge. Lead us to this guy's place. We'll do the rest. You can stay out of sight. No one will know it was you."

"His name is Manuel Garcia. And I don't want to stay away. I want to hurt him for what he did to my brother and for putting me in this position."

Better than I could've hoped for, Parkman thought.

"Then tell Daniel how to get to this guy's place, and we'll help you get your revenge."

Chapter 19

AARON HAD DRIFTED OFF. He woke once to urinate in the corner, saw through the cracks in the doorframe that the sun was still high, and went back to sleep. He wanted as much rest as possible for the escape this evening.

He rolled over, opened his eyes, and watched Casper sleeping as the light outside faded. He had doubts about tonight but suspected that fear was playing with him. Fear of the consequences he would face if he didn't get out of the compound. They already took one finger. If he didn't make it out, what would they take next? A foot? Or worse, a leg?

He didn't need a leg to stay alive while they waited to catch Sarah. They could torture him to within an inch of his life and still wait for Sarah. He had to find the determination on the inside like Sarah does. With Casper's help, he'd make it. But that also weighed on him. Casper's help meant Casper would pay dearly for that help.

He laid his head back and stared at the dark ceiling. How did he lose his courage, his zest for a fight? When did they break him?

Going through the events of how he came to be here, he couldn't pinpoint exactly when he lost his will to fight, but one thing was for sure—the fight inside him was coming back tenfold. He was angry with what they did to his hand. Angry at what they were doing to Sarah. Angry at everything. But he was angriest with himself for letting it get this far.

Spanish was a showman. He set up acts and played the scenes out using human beings as props. He intimidated, tortured, and killed people for his own gain. This was exactly the kind of man that Aaron detested. The kind of man Sarah would hospitalize or kill if needed.

Aaron hadn't mentioned to Casper that he wouldn't leave the compound without killing Spanish. Even if he had a clear break for the woods surrounding the property, he planned on staying long enough to kill Spanish. Aaron's life was different than Sarah's or Casper's. He ran a martial arts studio. He taught people self-defense. He didn't run in underworld circles, fighting and killing people. He wasn't a mercenary. But he'd make an exception with Spanish. That man needed to die, *should die*, as Sarah would say.

Casper stirred on the floor. He rolled onto his side and slowly got to his feet.

"You doing okay?" Aaron asked.

"Yeah. Just sleepy."

"Losing strength? Hungry?" Aaron sat up. "You sure we're doing the right thing here?"

"Yeah. You're leaving tonight. Tomorrow I'll eat your portion of the food and start feeling better."

Aaron didn't state what they both knew. If Aaron had successfully escaped tonight, Casper probably wouldn't have survived the night.

Just as Casper started to urinate in the same corner as Aaron did a few minutes before, footsteps sounded outside.

"They're coming," Aaron whispered.

Casper finished urinating, shook, tied his pants up, and turned around to face the door as the chains rattled outside.

Aaron checked the bandage over his wounded hand. It hadn't been changed since he swam in the reservoir. The tip of his finger itched, but he knew it wasn't there anymore. The gauze had thinned after being wet, and parts had stripped off. He'd tied the remaining bits tighter to keep the wound covered as best he could.

The door opened, and the last of the fading light filled the small cell.

"Get up," the man in the doorway ordered. "Come outside."

Aaron and Casper exchanged a look and started for the open door. Six men were gathered around, two on the periphery with machine guns cradled in their hands.

Spanish was not with them.

"The barn," the man closest to Aaron said.

They started off without being pushed or guided. At the barn door, an armed man on either side opened the large wooden doors slowly. A wave of trepidation slithered over Aaron as he willingly walked across the threshold. Images of drowning under the water torture flashed through his mind. The raw pain of the blade as it sliced his finger off.

"You okay?" Casper asked.

"No talking," one of the men barked.

"You've gone pale," Casper said, ignoring the warning.

A second passed before Casper was shoved from behind so hard that he sprawled forward and hit the barn's floor, where he slid several feet before stopping.

"Get up," the man ordered.

A defiant glare washed over Casper's face, then disappeared as fast as it materialized. Before anyone reached for him, Casper jumped to his feet and rejoined the throng headed to the center of the barn.

Four more men waited for them, armed to the teeth, Spanish standing between them. The four men looked like a SWAT team. They were decked out in combat gear, Kevlar vests with hand grenades dangling from their chests, and machine guns cradled in their hands.

Spanish appeared to be unarmed. With the firepower he possessed in the men guarding him, he didn't need a thing.

"Gentlemen," he said. "Come. Join me for a little demonstration."

Aaron was led to a wooden chair on the left and Casper to one on the right. Once seated, a man knelt and secured Aaron's ankles with duct tape. Then he did the same to Casper, leaving both their hands free.

Their escorts dropped back into the barn's darkened regions, leaving only Spanish and his four armed SWAT colleagues watching over their prisoners.

"I don't believe we've been formally introduced," Spanish said. "My name is Alejandro Gonzales. I work for Enzo Miguel Guzman or the Enzo Cartel. And I will be your executioner tonight."

Chapter 20

PARKMAN SAT BESIDE DANIEL as they pulled onto the residential street that led to Manuel Garcia's home. Daniel slowed the RV to a crawl on the dark street, then stopped two houses short of Manuel's gated front yard. The BMW SUV was parked just inside the gate as promised by the customs officer, Raúl. A few houses on the street had interior lights on, but the area was quiet otherwise.

Raúl sat on the bed in the back of the RV and added few details about Manuel other than to say that he was working for the devil—The Enzo Cartel—and was doing what he could to impress the cartel. Manuel's goal was to move up the ranks fast, as the Enzo Cartel was a relatively new one. Not one to waste time, Manuel used people like Raúl to do his dirty work. Raúl understood that if he got caught framing them with the drugs in their RV, it would be Raúl who got in trouble, not Manuel Garcia.

That was what got Raúl's brother killed.

Daniel got out of the driver's seat and headed to the back. Parkman pulled the curtains that enclosed the RV's front driver and passenger area. Then he followed Daniel to the rear to join the rest of them.

"What now?" Parkman asked.

Something had been bothering him since they had taken this side detour. It wasn't the story itself. It was a good story, and Raúl seemed sincere in the grief of losing his brother to Manuel's dealings. He couldn't quite put his finger on it yet, but something bothered him about Raúl's story in general. Maybe it was how fortunate they had been to have kidnapped the one customs officer who could lead them to an Enzo Cartel affiliate. Maybe that was all it was. He wasn't about to squander that gift, yet something still didn't feel quite right.

"He knows me," Raúl said, tapping his chest. "I go to the door. Knock. Tell him it worked. You're in trouble at the border. He will let me in. Then you all come in."

"I don't know." Benjamin shook his head. "If this is your friend, the door closes, and you disappear. Then what do we have?"

"No friend," Raúl pleaded. "No, friend. Hate him."

"Yeah, fine," Daniel said. "But we don't trust you."

"No friend," he repeated.

Parkman exchanged a look with Daniel, then met Alex's eyes.

"What do you guys want to do?" Parkman asked. "We're no closer to finding Sarah or Aaron. We're floundering around here with a kidnapped customs officer who tried to frame us, and the authorities are probably looking for this RV as we speak. The dark will shield us a little, but we can't be in this RV come tomorrow morning. Do we steal a car, leave this guy tied up somewhere, and keep driving around aimlessly looking for a cartel? Or hope this guy is telling us the truth?"

"It is, it is," Raúl broke in. "The truth."

"Shhh." Parkman held a finger to his lips. "What's the verdict, guys?"

"Go forward with Raúl's plan," Daniel said. "But at any point, be ready to fight or break and run if it doesn't work out."

Parkman looked at Alex, who nodded his agreement. Benjamin nodded, too.

He turned to Raúl. "You better pray you're telling us the truth."

"It is, Señor. It is the truth."

"Will the gate be unlocked?" Parkman asked.

Raúl shrugged. "I don't know. But I can use the buzzer—what you call it—doorbell."

"Suit up, boys. Let's go tie this guy up and take his ride. It's a bit ironic that one of Enzo's falcones will be the one that leads us to him and in his own vehicle."

"Yeah, ironic," Daniel mumbled.

Parkman detected by the look on Daniel's face that he wasn't buying what Raúl was saying either. What else could they do? Drive away? Stay in the RV? Steal a random car?

Even if Raúl weren't on the up and up, at least they'd be taking the vehicle of his associate, so there was that.

This trip had been tainted since they started. Breaking Parkman out of the safe house was risky and stupid. They didn't need him on this trip. Aaron's teachers could've crossed the border and stayed in the RV the whole time without this unwanted attention. Now they had kidnapped him, crossed into Mexico with him, and kidnapped a customs officer. Short of turning themselves in—which they wouldn't do in Mexico—they had to keep moving forward and see where it took them.

Sarah would.

Parkman pulled the curtain at the front and stared at Manuel's house for a full minute.

"Okay. We go. There's no sign of movement. Raúl, you take the lead. Alex, step outside first and disappear but stay close."

The door opened and swung shut.

Alex was gone.

"Daniel, leave the keys in the ignition in case we need to bolt. Benjamin, come with me and stay close to Raúl. Cool?"

Parkman let the curtain fall back in place. The boys nodded.

Parkman turned to Raúl. "Let's go get your revenge."

Raúl moved for the door without a sound; Benjamin close behind him.

Parkman leaned down to Daniel and whispered. "If this goes bad in there, pull up to the house and leave the door open. We may need to exit this area faster than we arrived."

"Got it." Daniel slapped Parkman on the shoulder. "Just get the keys to that SUV."

Parkman left the RV and closed the door quietly. Benjamin and Raúl waited on the sidewalk. He joined them, and as a trio, they headed down two houses to Manuel's white gate.

Parkman could almost feel Daniel's eyes on him. Alex's too. These were good guys. He didn't want them stained with violence or murder. The underbelly of society was rough to take and colored your impression of humanity once exposed to it. You can never reclaim your innocence. You can never un-see something, undo something. Once you've seen it, killed it, consumed it, *it* became you. Some were comfortable with *it*, like Sarah. Others were scarred by *it* forever.

At the gate, the RV suddenly seemed very far away. None of the boys had weapons. Parkman had thought the idea of having a couple of guns was good, but the boys didn't want to kill anyone so savagely. If a death was needed, they all knew how to kill with their hands very efficiently.

Raúl hit the buzzer at the gate and waited. He didn't appear to be any more or less nervous than inside the RV, but Parkman was having trouble reading him. This could go either way, and right now, to boost morale, they needed this to go their way.

Raúl buzzed again.

"Yeah?" a gruff male voice answered. "Who's there?"

"It's Raúl. Let me in."

There was silence for a moment. Then, "Who's with you?"

"Reclutas."

Benjamin smacked Raúl's arm and whispered, "What's that mean?"

Parkman leaned in close to Benjamin. "It means recruits," he said, keeping his voice low. "He's brought us to see if there's a job we can handle for Manuel."

The gate buzzed open. Parkman followed Raúl as he moved to the side of the house and headed for the door halfway to the backyard. The gate closed behind them with finality. He looked back, but the street was deserted. An outside light flicked on as they approached the side door. All they could do now was ride this wave in.

The door opened. A large man, about twenty-five years old, a bandanna covering his bald pate, stepped outside and looked Raúl up and down.

"What the fuck you come here for, Ese?"

"They forced me to," Raúl said and stepped closer to Manuel.

"Hey," Parkman said as he felt Benjamin go rigid beside him. "Take it easy."

Raúl turned around and pointed at Parkman. "No, you take it easy. You're da one who is fucked now."

"Alex," Parkman shouted. "Raúl lied. Abort."

He turned around and faced two men holding handguns behind them.

"What's this?" he asked even as he understood. Coming to the side door allowed these guys to exit the house at the front and come around behind them. The slight delay at the gate gave them time to get armed and into position.

Raúl had tried to set them up at the border. When that didn't work, he did it again. This time he did a better job. Parkman could slap himself for believing Raúl's fabricated tale, but the sudden movement would probably get him killed.

"Inside," Manuel said behind them. "We got a little business to discuss in the basement."

Parkman had no play. He glanced at Benjamin, who seemed to figure the same thing.

He turned slowly and headed for the open side door. As he passed Raúl, the customs officer drove a sucker punch across Parkman's cheek. He narrowly missed braining himself against the doorframe with the sudden whip of his head to the side.

"That's for fucking up my job. Now I got to call them and tell them I was sick or something. They're going to want an explanation. Why the hell would I just walk away from my job?" Raúl punched Parkman in the side. "You asshole!"

Benjamin stepped up beside him. Parkman waved him off as he stood up and met Raúl's glare.

"You won't live through the night," Parkman stated in an even voice.

"Get them to the basement," Manuel shouted. "Now!"

Parkman stepped inside and started downstairs. Benjamin followed with one of the gunmen coming down behind him.

From the side door, Parkman heard Manuel tell the other gunman to use his sound suppressor on his weapon when he killed the driver waiting in the RV.

"Also, there's another one," Raúl said. "A short skinny one named Alex. He's watching the house somewhere. Find him. Kill him. But bring me something. A hand, an arm. I don't care. Cut something off and bring it to me. I need something to show Enzo. Now go."

The side door closed.

Raúl locked it and started down the stairs.

Chapter 21

AARON RESTED HIS WOUNDED hand across his thighs as he watched Spanish—Alejandro Gonzales—open a box that sat on the table between him and Casper. Both men heard Alejandro say loudly that he would be their executioner. Did he mean he would kill them tonight? Was this the end? Had the Enzo Cartel tired of them, or had they caught Sarah?

He would have to wait and see. While waiting, he would watch for an opening and do something about leaving this place. In any good sparring in Shotokan karate, you watch for an opening, a hole in your opponent's defense, and strike. It was what he was used to, what he knew. It was what he would do tonight.

"Inside this box," Alejandro started, "I have a very special gift for the both of you." He glanced in the open box, then turned back to Aaron. "But first, I would like to update you both."

An office chair was wheeled in from the side. Alejandro sat and reclined backward. As before, one large light, a naked bulb, hung suspended from the barn roof, illuminating their immediate area, but everything outside the light's grasp was cast in darkness.

They waited for him to speak. Aaron's stomach roiled around, and a cool sheen of sweat had broken out over his body. He glanced at Casper, who seemed to be calm. Casper stared into the darkness, glanced left, averted his eyes from something, looked up, then down, and met Aaron's eyes. He winked, then continued his examination of the barn.

Behind Alejandro, a man stepped into view and handed him a drink and a phone. Alejandro listened on the phone and handed it back.

The man disappeared in the gloom behind Alejandro's chair.

"I've been told that certain friends of yours have come to Mexico to find you, Aaron."

Friends?

"Three young men and an older male. Daniel, Benjamin, and Alex. Also, a man named Parkman."

"What?" Aaron stood up from his seat so fast he almost fell because he momentarily forgot his feet were secured with duct tape. A hand slapped down on his shoulder and rammed him back into the hard wooden seat.

"Don't worry about your friends anymore, Aaron." Alejandro sipped the amber liquid in his glass and then offered a sardonic smile to Aaron. "They are being taken care of as we speak." Alejandro turned to Casper, then back to Aaron. "Your little rescue didn't pan out too well, did it?"

Aaron fought the urge to call Alejandro every name he

could think of. They were so tough with their gunmen and their small army. If they could go one-on-one, he would see how long Alejandro could keep that smug look on his face.

Alejandro spun his office chair in a circle and then planted his feet to stop as soon as it faced Aaron again.

"Sarah met with an accident today."

Aaron's heart almost stopped in his chest. "You will die," he whispered through his tightened jaw.

"What was that? Speak up."

Pent-up fury forced its way through Aaron, and he shouted the same three words. He leaned forward as far as he could, heat rising to his face.

"I'm sure I will die one day." Alejandro laughed and drank more liquid from his glass. "But I doubt I'm the one dying today. Although, we're getting off-topic. We aren't here to discuss my death. We're here to discuss Sarah's and yours." He waved a finger between the two men.

Aaron's head spun as he felt lightheaded. He was reeling with an insane fury. How did it get this far?

"What happened to Sarah?" Casper asked.

Casper's voice broke through Aaron's attention on Alejandro. He breathed in deep, lowered his eyes to the barn's dirt floor, and waited to hear what Alejandro would say next.

"Sarah was a passenger in a Hummer when it was hit by a dump truck on the passenger side." Alejandro paused to drink.

Aaron breathed deeply, holding his tongue.

"No one has been able to locate the driver. I've been informed that Sarah is now in the hospital with a cracked ribcage. She's currently under police guard."

Casper was probably wondering the same thing Aaron was. What the hell was Sarah doing in a Hummer? And who had she been with?

Alejandro got up from his office chair. "Consider your friends dead. They're locked in a basement and about to be killed this minute. I have men going to the hospital to pick up Sarah and bring her here." He looked at his watch. "As soon as the police guards change shifts at eleven this evening, our man comes on duty. Then we take Sarah. But you won't see her as we don't need either of you anymore."

He walked over to the box on the table and set his glass down. He reached inside the box and withdrew something that resembled an oven mitt. Alejandro turned it over in his hands.

"I heard you two discussing your pathetic escape plan." He looked at Aaron. "I found it interesting that you called me Spanish. I thought, hey, you should know my name before I kill you." He set the glove on the table and removed another. "We're not stupid down here. We have listening devices in your little cell that make parabolic devices pale in comparison. We hear everything and can even decipher mumbling under your breath." He shrugged. "Who knows when a prisoner feels like talking to a fellow inmate? Why else would I put you two together?"

Aaron looked over at Casper. His eyes weren't as calm anymore. He seemed despondent. Like this was the end. Tied up and surrounded by so many armed men, it seemed hope would be fleeting, yet Aaron still had some. What else was there? Death or hope. He would have hope as long as he was still breathing—until death was absolute. Only hope can beat the devil. Hope was greater than fear.

"This glove is a masterpiece." Alejandro held one up and turned it over in his hand. "Have you ever heard of a bullet ant?"

Aaron didn't respond. Neither did Casper.

Alejandro continued as if he hadn't asked them a question. "A bullet ant looks like a reddish brown wingless wasp. They hail from the rainforests of Nicaragua. Their sting is so bad and painful that it feels like you've been shot, hence the name, *bullet* ant."

Aaron squirmed in his chair. Was the box filled with bullet ants, and the glove was the only protection? What was Alejandro up to? Was he going to torture them to death?

Alejandro picked up his drink and finished the beverage off. "They're also called the 24-hour ant because the pain, waves of burning, throbbing pain, remains unabated for twenty-four hours without relief. There's a stupid tribe in South America called the Satere-Mawe tribe. After sedating bullet ants, they weave them into a glove made of leaves, just like these two here."

The ants weren't in the box. The ants were in the gloves. Aaron's body weakened at the thought of putting that glove on.

"This tribe," Alejandro continued, "makes a tribe member put the gloves on for at least ten minutes while being repeatedly bitten by what some consider the most painful bite of any insect in the world. This is a test of manhood and a test to become a warrior for the tribe. They do this exercise up to twenty times over several months, per person." Alejandro picked up one of the gloves and walked over to Casper. "You two are the lucky ones. You only have to wear the glove on one hand each, and you only have to do it once."

He set the glove down on the table by Casper. Then walked over and placed the other glove by Aaron.

"Now, don't worry. The bite will cause paralysis, but that's only temporary. It's something to do with the venom interfering with your central nervous system. But in about thirty minutes, neither of you will ever need to worry about your central nervous system, or any other system for that matter, ever again."

"What is this all for?" Casper asked. His voice didn't waver or crack. He seemed quite calm. "Why do this?"

"Because I enjoy watching a man's pain threshold laid out for all to see. If there were a God, he wouldn't have created us to deal with as much pain as the human body has to endure throughout our lives. Since there is no God, that means there's no devil. This is it." He waved his hands around. "This one life. This is all we have, and only the strong survive. Not only do I like killing off my enemy, but I also enjoy watching them endure pain. I think they call people like me a sadist, but that's sorely misunderstood. I enjoy causing pain. It's good for the soul."

"That's what being a sadist is."

Alejandro shook his head. "See? Misunderstood." He moved closer to Casper and smacked the table. "No more questions. Place the glove on your hand or be flayed."

"Flayed?"

"I've done it before. I've skinned a man just to watch him bleed. I think the glove is a better alternative. Do it now, before the ants wake from their sleep."

Aaron stared across the table at Casper, wondering what he would do. As much as he wanted to grasp at hope, it was certainly fleeting. Adrenaline flowed through his blood, and he shook uncontrollably, yet Casper seemed calm.

Then Casper surprised him. He picked up the glove, slid his hand inside, and placed it back on the table to wait.

Alejandro clapped. "Well done. This ought to be good." He turned to the guard on Casper's right. "I've always wanted to see what happens when bullet ants start biting—"

Casper shouted so abruptly and loudly that Aaron jumped from his seat. Even Alejandro, the tough cartel man, jumped and stared at Casper.

He held his hand up in front of his eyes and yelled like he was in the worst pain known to mankind while Alejandro leaned in close and studied Casper's face.

In Aaron's peripheral vision, he noticed both guards on either side of him had stepped closer to get a better look as Casper yelled. The wail, as well as Alejandro's safety, had drawn them too close to Aaron.

Aaron looked at the Kevlar vests and the guns the men held. The grenades strapped to their vests dangled from their individual clips. Everyone watched Casper as his face reddened with the screaming.

They were dead no matter how this played out. It wouldn't be without pain, as evidenced by Casper's shouting. Aaron decided it would be better to die fast and go out fighting than to sit around in the cartel's barn being tortured.

Aaron lunged to the left with his good hand, snapped a grenade off the guy's vest, brought the pin to his mouth, bit it out, and tossed it hard at Casper's chair, where it rolled between the legs and out behind the chair where two other guards stood. As he lunged for another grenade before the guy beside him stepped away, he prayed the delay from pulling the pin was at least ten seconds. Otherwise, he was going to blow Casper up.

The men in the room all reacted differently. One guard behind Casper shouted something, which was drowned out by Casper's inhuman hollering. Alejandro stepped away from Casper and pivoted to see what Aaron was doing.

The guard to Aaron's right leveled his weapon at Aaron as he pulled the second pin with his teeth.

Simultaneously, Aaron launched himself backward as the man fired.

The guards behind Casper were running away as Casper whipped the glove off his hand and dove toward Alejandro.

The first grenade exploded behind Casper's chair.

The sound stunned Aaron as he landed on his back, using his body to land hard and break the chair, but it didn't give.

The guard he had yanked the grenades off had been shot by the guard on Aaron's right. It all happened so fast.

Aaron still held the other grenade but was trapped like a turtle on his back; his feet held firm to the chair with duct tape.

Alejandro shouted for someone to get Casper off of him.

The guard on the left dropped to his knees, blood pulsing from a bullet wound. Aaron needed the man's weapon. He passed the grenade with no pin into his wounded hand, carefully keeping the firing mechanism depressed. Before the guard collapsed completely, Aaron snatched a handgun from the man's waistband. He brought it to his face, panting frantically, shaking, and flipped the safety off.

When he spun his head to the right, the other guard was gone. After mistakenly shooting his colleague, he had gone to help get Casper off Alejandro.

Aaron aimed his shaking hand as best he could, then

fired.

The bullet tore a hole in the guard's neck, an inch above the Kevlar. He couldn't have asked for a better spot.

The man reeled off Casper and stumbled backward, holding his neck as blood seeped out.

Then Aaron aimed at Alejandro and realized he wasn't holding the grenade in his wounded hand anymore. It had rolled out without him noticing and sat two feet to his right.

Even as he aimed the weapon between his ankles, he assumed the grenade would kill him before he had a chance to escape. But he fired at the duct tape anyway, tearing it in half. His ankles were free.

Footsteps stampeded in from outside.

Aaron did a backflip off the chair as he threw himself at the wounded guard on his left. He landed on the man, and without losing his grip on the gun, he hugged the man close and rolled, putting the man's body between him and the inevitable explosion of the grenade.

Just as he was about to be covered by the guard, four armed men rushed up and stood in front of the table, right in front of the grenade.

Aaron didn't have time to check on Casper, but he hoped he would take cover as well.

The grenade exploded. The body on him jolted from the pressure. Aaron lost his ability to hear. A ringing sensation clung to his ears.

Wearily, he pushed the man off and raised the gun. When he saw no immediate threat, he sat up. The four men who had run up to the table were sprawled on the floor, two of them still moving. Blood was everywhere. Pieces of torn clothing, chunks of flesh, and crimson liquid covered the scene. It all happened in less than a minute, too fast to comprehend anything other than survival.

Aaron got to his feet, the torn duct tape still attached to each ankle. He walked over to Alejandro and aimed the weapon at the back of his head.

Alejandro was thrust aside a second later, and Aaron looked down at Casper's smiling face. Casper's mouth moved, but Aaron couldn't hear what he was saying.

Aaron touched his ears and gestured that he couldn't hear.

Casper offered a thumbs up, then ripped at the duct tape on his ankles.

Aaron turned and studied the scene. The guards who had stood behind Casper were unconscious or dead from the first grenade. His guards were dead, and it appeared Alejandro had died from the second grenade blast when Casper hugged him as protection.

The four men who ran in to help Alejandro had stood right over the grenade. In less than a minute, they had killed and wounded eight men, including Alejandro.

Now they just needed to leave the building without being killed and get to the hospital to save Sarah.

"You in there," someone shouted.

Aaron heard that like it was coming down a tunnel, muffled through doorways. His hearing was coming back. He glanced at Casper, who had also heard the voice.

"We have the barn surrounded. Put down your weapons and come out. We'll burn the barn to the ground if we don't see you within five minutes."

Aaron looked at Casper. He was smiling.

"Good job," Casper yelled.

Aaron nodded his thanks.

"Let's kill us a few more cartel guys. You with me?"

Aaron nodded again and wiped something off his face. Blood. Someone's blood was all over him.

"Get as many weapons as you can off these guys," Casper said as he began snatching guns and grenades off the man Aaron had shot in the throat.

"Then we kill everyone outside," he said.

"Aren't you hurt from that glove?" Aaron asked when he found his voice.

"No," Casper shook his head. "The ants were still sedated. I yelled like that as a diversion, hoping you'd do something. I had no idea you'd turn it into a scene from Rambo or some shit. That was intense. We need guys like you where I work."

It was Aaron's turn to smile.

Chapter 22

Sarah settled in at the hospital. They had done X-rays and determined three ribs were cracked, but she had no internal bleeding or other injuries. She didn't understand why they gave her an IV drip for cracked ribs. She hated hospitals, and being guarded by Mexican authorities in a Mexican hospital was not boding well for her. Darwin needed her to stay and wait for the cartel to come, but she kept thinking about ways to leave this place.

Without a knock, the door opened.

Her special nurse, her *demanding* nurse, an American working in Mexico, was sassy and smart. Tessa McCurry, with a strong maternal instinct, made Sarah listen.

"How are you feeling?" Tessa asked as she approached the bed.

"Like I got run *over* by the truck and not just hit by it." Sarah pointed at the white padding they'd wrapped around her ribs. "Is this necessary? It restricts my breathing, and this constant tightness in my chest adds to the pain."

Tessa raised her eyebrows. "If it weren't necessary, we wouldn't have used it." She adjusted Sarah's bedsheets, even though Sarah had kicked them off earlier because it was too hot. "We don't do things unnecessarily here." Then she let out a short, choked-off laugh.

"I wasn't implying—"

"I understand," Tessa cut her off. "And I'm abundantly clear that it is necessary." She stepped away from the bed and picked up Sarah's chart. "You should be out of here in the morning." She set the clipboard down and moved toward the door. "When you leave, you can do whatever you want with that wrap. But not before. We clear on that point?"

There was a hint of a smile in Tessa's voice.

"Clear," Sarah said. Then added, "Abundantly."

Tessa opened the door and slipped into the hall without another word.

Sarah kicked the covers off and moaned as pain flared up.

Suddenly Vivian was there. She swooped into her consciousness. Sarah's head shot backward at the surprise interruption.

"Whoa …" she whispered. "Thanks for stopping by, stranger."

Vivian ignored Sarah's sarcasm and stated that a group of women were coming to see her and that this group of women needed to gain access to her room. Sarah had to clear it with the police guard watching her door. If the group didn't meet Sarah, then she would die in Mexico. The cartel would succeed in killing her. Meeting this group of women would save her life.

"But how?" Sarah asked, the pit in her stomach turning over.

Just meet them. I can't lose you ...

Sarah shouted for the police guard. He didn't respond. Ignoring the pain, she shouted again.

Chapter 23

THE MAN HOPPED A fence, then another. He stayed close to the houses. When he got to one that contained a guard dog, he nonchalantly used the sidewalk, then stopped behind a tree.

Daniel watched the man's progress from the passenger side window, where the curtain offered him an inch to look out through. In the dark, it was impossible for anyone to notice him from the outside. His hands clenched, then unclenched as he waited for the man behind the tree to do something.

It felt wrong. Being here. Raúl had set them up somehow. He just knew it. Why was a man sneaking up on the RV if he hadn't set them up?

The silhouette of the man eased out from behind the tree. The meager streetlight bounced off something metal in his hand.

Daniel unlocked the RV's door quietly and eased

backward, careful not to shake the vehicle. He continued through the RV until he got to the bathroom, where he turned the light on. Then he closed the bathroom door softly and headed into the bedroom, where he took refuge on the bed behind the wall.

He waited.

It took a maddening three minutes before Daniel heard the familiar click of the front passenger side door unlatching as it was opened. He waited, his eyes closed, focusing on the man's sounds. He waited for anything that would alert him to how close the man was getting.

His stomach flitted with the energy of excitement. The excitement of sparring was something Aaron had trained his teachers to do well. They were his best students and diligently trained for this sort of dangerous confrontation without ever having the chance—or ever wanting to—encounter such a situation as this one.

He breathed calmly, quietly, and listened. The man was careful as he entered the RV. He didn't allow his clothes to touch anything, to get snagged. He stayed balanced. Walked on the carpeted floor, testing his step before applying his weight. Daniel ascertained all that from the man's movements, his breathing, which was rapid and frightened. There was a subtle movement in the RV as the man stopped in front of the bathroom door.

Daniel prepared to spring into action as his leg muscles were beginning to cramp. The intruder had taken his time. Time Daniel didn't want to waste if his friends inside the house needed him.

The man ripped open the bathroom door, shouted something nonsensical, and fired his weapon.

Daniel leaped off the bed, landed in a crouch behind the open bathroom door, then slammed into it with his shoulder, driving the door into the guy and knocking the intruder to the floor.

But it didn't dislodge the gun from his hand. The guy spun to see what had hit him and brought the gun around as he adjusted himself on the floor.

Frantic that at any second he'd be shot, Daniel dove for the guy, going for the gun.

The weapon fired.

Chapter 24

Parkman stared at Raúl with rage. He schooled himself that the kind of rage he felt would get himself killed if he didn't take a few breaths and wait to see what happened next.

He was worried for Daniel, who had a gunman heading his way without Daniel knowing it. And what happened to Alex? He was supposed to be watching the house.

The basement opened to sliding doors at the back leading out to a well-groomed backyard. Pool lights lit the rim of a kidney-shaped pool with a rock waterfall near the back. The grass and concrete walkway surrounding the pool were in immaculate shape. If this was Manuel's house, the guy made good money. Drug money. Cartel money.

"Bring them into this room," Manuel said.

Raúl gestured with a nod of his head.

Parkman met Benjamin's eyes and tried to relay the message to be ready. Do nothing yet, but be ready.

Parkman got to the door of the next room and stopped. The windowless room had no furniture. It was covered wall to wall in thick plastic. A large tub was hooked into the plumbing at the back of the room where an old bathroom once was.

A dead body disposal room.

"Move," Raúl said, jamming something sharp into Parkman's back.

Parkman stepped inside the room. Tools were suspended from the wall on either side of the entrance. Two saws, forceps, knives with serrated edges, swords, and other cutting devices. None of them were very clean. There was a roll of duct tape, rope, and even a set of brass knuckles.

This was a torture-death room.

Raúl flicked on a floodlight.

Then Parkman saw the rest and understood immediately. Each wall was coated with a thick foamy material. Soundproofing. Once the door was closed, no one outside the house would hear a thing as they tortured people at will down there. They could shower off in the tub and wrap the plastic up for trash day.

He couldn't let the door close. If he did, they would never see the light of day again.

"Wait," he said.

Manuel shook his head. "No, there's nothing to wait for."

A weapon fired from outside somewhere.

"What was that?" Raúl asked. He exchanged a glance with Manuel. "Your boys need guns against these unarmed kids?"

The weapon fired again.

"Shit, man," Manuel growled. "Don't need this kind of

aggravation where I live."

He stormed across the room, bumped Benjamin's shoulder, and stopped at the door. "Get these two ready. I'll be right back."

"Remember, we need proof," Raúl said. "Decapitate them or take a hand. But get something."

Manuel nodded and slammed the door closed.

Parkman's stomach dropped as he glanced at Benjamin, who seemed to be taking all this like it was a joke, a prank.

Raúl locked the door without taking his eyes off them.

"Take your shirts off."

"Fuck you," Benjamin said. "You want my shirt off? Come do it yourself."

"How about this? I kill you, then take your shirt off?"

"It's the only way you're getting my shirt."

"Fine."

Raúl raised the gun, aimed at Benjamin's chest, and fired.

Chapter 25

Daniel didn't feel any pain, nor did he focus on it. All he needed to do was subdue the man under him, remove all weapons, and ask him what was happening in the house.

He snapped the guy's wrist back until he bellowed and dropped the gun. Then Daniel jammed the guy's wrist into the wall beside them, where he heard bones snap. The guy's scream changed pitch.

Daniel raised a knee into the man's crotch while punching him in the sternum with enough force to drive the wind from the guy's lungs.

With his wrist dangling at an odd angle, the man brought his legs up and tried to turn on his side as he struggled to breathe.

Daniel allowed him the turn and took a second to collect his breath while roving his body in search of a bullet hole. He found nothing. When he looked up, there was a small hole in the RV's roof near where the ceiling connected with the wall. Based on that angle, the guy hadn't gotten the gun in place in time before he had taken the shot.

He got down on one knee, punched the man's broken wrist, and grabbed his hair as the man screeched with what little breath he was getting now.

"What's happening in the house?" Daniel barked.

He mumbled something, but Daniel couldn't get it.

"What was that?" Daniel asked, his fist poised above the guy's face.

"Dead. They're all dead." He breathed in deeply like he was sucking air through a thin pipe. "Dead. Like you."

Daniel dropped his fist so hard the man's head bounced off the floor. Then he hit him again. And again.

It took him a moment to gather that his assailant had been knocked out.

He retrieved the man's gun from the carpeted floor, stashed it at the back of his waistband, and got to his feet. Once outside, he ran close to the fence, approaching the house while keeping an eye on the neighborhood. Someone had to have heard the gunfire. Someone would be calling the police.

If they were all dead, Daniel would have no choice. He would have to murder everyone in the house.

Daniel just prayed the guy in the RV was wrong and that he still had time.

Chapter 26

BENJAMIN UNDERSTOOD RAÚL'S INTENT the second the trigger was being depressed. He twisted his shoulders as Raúl fired, but he wasn't faster than a bullet. Parkman saw the blood fly out the backside of Benjamin's shoulder, spraying the plastic behind him.

Then he fell, shock filling his eyes as he became aware he'd been shot. Parkman stood paralyzed in the aftermath.

"Move away from him," Raúl ordered.

Parkman stepped toward Benjamin.

"I said, *move away*."

The gun appeared in Parkman's face, drawing him up straight. The cordite was still fresh, the fear raw.

"Walk to the tub in the corner. Step in it. Then don't move."

Benjamin squirmed on the floor as blood oozed out of his body.

"Do it now," Raúl said, his voice taking on a hardened quality.

Parkman watched Benjamin as he took his first step backward. It was over for them. They were alone in this plastic room with a gunman and had no play. How did he let it get this far? It was his fault Benjamin got shot. All this was his fault.

"It's okay," Benjamin grunted. "Don't get shot on account of me. Do what he says. Alex and Daniel will be here shortly."

Parkman took another step backward. Then he turned and stepped inside the tub. Benjamin had a growing circle of blood under him, his face white and creased at the eyes as he tried to manage the pain.

Raúl circled Benjamin, knelt beside him, being mindful of watching Parkman, and punched him in the side of the face.

"Your friends aren't coming." Raúl looked up at Parkman. "See what happens when you don't listen? Now take your shirt off." He glanced up at Parkman. "You move out of that tub, and I will shoot you in the balls. You won't die right away, but man, the pain."

Raúl grabbed the bottom of Benjamin's shirt and went to lift it up when, with a burst of speed barely caught by Parkman's eye, Benjamin shot a contorted fist across Raúl's chest and into the hand holding the weapon. Instantly Raúl's wrist went limp, the gun dropping to aim at the floor.

Benjamin twisted up, slapped something in Raúl's underarm, and his entire arm dropped limp beside him.

"What did you do to my arm?" Raúl shouted.

Benjamin laid back down, shot his fist up, and did the

same to the other arm as Parkman launched out of the tub. He barreled across the plastic-covered room and dove on Raúl, dropping all his weight on the man. Under him, Raúl grunted and squirmed, but his arms were temporarily paralyzed.

Parkman punched Raúl half a dozen times before he stopped. When he eased off, panting like he'd run a hundred-meter dash, Raúl had a newly broken nose, shattered lips as they had ground on his teeth under Parkman's fists, and blood seeping from his left eye.

It had happened so fast. All Parkman understood was movement and action. Benjamin had attacked. Then Parkman attacked.

It was over. Benjamin needed a hospital.

Someone knocked on the door.

"Hey, open up."

Parkman grabbed Raúl's gun off the floor, moved to the wall where he yanked the roll of duct tape off its hook, and tossed it toward Benjamin.

"It's Alex and Daniel. Open up."

Parkman blew out the breath he'd been holding, reached for the lock, and then stopped.

"You alone?" he asked.

"Our house guests are tied up," he heard through the door.

Parkman turned the latch and stepped aside, keeping the gun where it would work best for him.

The door opened, and Alex and Daniel walked in.

"What happened here?" Daniel asked, looking over at Raúl's ruined face. His eyes moved to Parkman's bloody knuckles, then Benjamin's shoulder.

"Raúl shot Benjamin. Benjamin attacked Raúl. I hit him

a few times. What happened upstairs?"

"One of them approached the trailer," Daniel said. "Shot a couple new holes in it. He's out cold. This is his weapon."

"I watched you guys walk around to the side of the house," Alex said. "Two armed men came out the front door and circled in behind you. I slipped inside the house through the open front door when they were preoccupied with you. All other people, even that guy Manuel, are out cold." Alex reached into his pocket and pulled out the car keys. "And I have the keys to the BMW SUV."

"Guys?" Benjamin grunted from the floor. "Bit of help here."

"Shit." Parkman dropped to Benjamin's side and grabbed the duct tape. "Someone, hold him up. We need to stop this bleeding."

Daniel and Alex got down by Benjamin's shoulders and gently lifted him as Parkman applied three pieces of tape to the open wound in his shoulder blade.

"What did you do to Raúl's arms?" Parkman asked.

"Special nerve inside the underarm," Benjamin said with a surprisingly strong voice for being shot. "Momentary paralysis of the arm."

"Why did you tempt him so much?" Parkman asked.

Benjamin turned white with the pain. His jaw muscles protruded on either side.

"Mistake. Didn't think he'd shoot."

"Come on? In this room? Covered in plastic and soundproofed? Why wouldn't he?"

"Mistook him for a pussy. All talk. No bite. The second I realized I was wrong, I tried"—he coughed and then groaned —"I tried to spin away. Caught my shoulder."

"I'd have done the same," Alex quipped.

"It's done now," Parkman said. He nodded at Benjamin. "We have to carry you out. It might hurt …"

"Just do it."

"Okay, Nike."

Parkman took Benjamin's ankles and went to lift him when Alex motioned for him to stop.

"One second."

Alex and Daniel removed their shirts and tied the sleeves together expertly. Gently lifting Benjamin's head, they slipped the sleeves under his upper body and brought their respective shirts out from under Benjamin's armpits, effectively placing his back in a sling.

"Good thinking."

Parkman grabbed Benjamin's ankles, and each man lifted their side of the sling. As a threesome, they walked Benjamin out of the basement, along the sidewalk, and gently placed him inside the RV on the bed in the back, stepping over Manuel's thug to do it.

When Benjamin was settled in the bed, Daniel grabbed the thug's feet and dragged him outside, his head bumping each step until he hit the concrete. Then he dragged him up to the fence and left him there.

Back inside the RV, they pooled the weapons they had taken along with the car keys from the BMW.

"Alex, can you follow in the Beemer?" Parkman asked.

"Yes."

"Good. Do that. Stay close. I'll GPS a hospital and direct Daniel. We have to get Benjamin patched up. There's no other way."

"We'll be arrested," Daniel said.

"It's the only way to keep Benjamin alive."

"Then we go." Daniel dropped in the driver's seat, and Alex disappeared outside to drive the BMW.

If there was one thing he loved about these guys, it was their discipline. And trust. He was close to Sarah, who was close to Aaron. When he said there was no chance, they sprang into action without protest, without whining. He needed men like this in his life. Men he could count on. Men who could help him investigate missing people and cheating spouses. The usual shit he saw come through his private firm.

He also loved that these guys would take a punch for each other.

Or a bullet.

He checked Benjamin's pulse as Daniel pulled out onto the street.

"Where's that hospital?" Daniel shouted back.

Parkman pulled his phone out. "I'm on it."

They drove away from the horror house where they were supposed to die, no closer to finding Sarah and Aaron.

They drove away, losing hope with each mile.

Chapter 27

AARON GOT HIMSELF SET up by the barn's side door as the loudspeaker outside repeated their demands.

Casper wanted to walk right out the front door of the barn. It was Aaron's job to create a diversion at the side.

They had duct-taped Alejandro's body to the office chair. Casper had gently stuck a grenade under Alejandro's butt at the side door, minus the pin. Then he'd found a black hood and placed it over Alejandro's head.

They were ready.

"One minute and we burn the place down," the man outside said.

"Coming out," Casper shouted.

Aaron's heart was in his throat. They had no idea how many men they would encounter outside. There could be two or three, or two or three hundred. Whatever there was, they would die inside for sure. Breaking out of the barn had the best odds of survival.

"You ready?" Casper whispered to Aaron.

He nodded. "Locked and loaded."

"You know what to do?"

Aaron nodded again.

Casper lifted the wooden bar that locked the side door.

"Coming out," he shouted. "We are not armed. Don't shoot."

"Thirty seconds."

He shoved open the door and let it swing around, where it bumped into the outer wall of the barn.

"We've got a prisoner. Alejandro is in the chair. If you shoot us, he dies."

"No deal."

Casper met Aaron's gaze. "What the hell?" He turned to the open door. "You fire on us, and you will kill Alejandro."

"We take orders from him," came the reply. "Alejandro, you there?"

"He's unconscious."

"No deal."

Aaron smacked Casper's arm. "Now what?"

"Roll him out. Then we run for the front door as they fixate on him."

Aaron nodded and pushed the chair, keeping himself inside the barn. It rolled smoothly on the concrete, out the side door opening, and stopped about four feet from them.

"There," Casper shouted. "Come take him. All we want is safe passage." It was his turn to smack Aaron's arm. "Let's go."

They sprinted across the dirty floor of the barn carrying what weapons they had salvaged and made it to the large double doors before they heard the explosion. Someone had moved Alejandro, and now Alejandro was in a thousand pieces, and whoever tried to move him was dead.

Casper pulled the barn's front door open enough to slip through, moved sideways, and ducked alongside the barn's outer wall.

"Over here," someone shouted.

Aaron dove through the door as gunfire tore into the wood above his head.

Casper fired his weapon toward the muzzle flashes. He raked the area, waited a moment, then raked it again.

Whatever he did had silenced the shooter. Aaron unclipped a grenade and pulled the pin. He slipped along the wall until he came to the corner. With his awkward left hand, he threw the grenade over his head.

Then he rejoined Casper by the wall, and together they started for the stables where the horses were riled up, whinnying in their stalls.

The explosion behind them was welcoming. They were leaving a trail of destruction. It was an accomplishment Aaron thought he'd never see just hours ago.

How many men were at the compound? Aaron ran the numbers through his head. With Alejandro and eight of his team dead inside the barn and a few more outside, that made about a dozen men. The rest of the security for the Enzo Cartel could be out hunting Sarah and managing business interests. They hadn't met Enzo himself yet, either.

It allowed him a smidgen of hope. Maybe they would get out together tonight. He hated the thought of leaving Casper behind.

At the stables, hoping no one would fire on them in fear

of hitting the equestrian beauties Enzo had no doubt spent a fortune on, Casper and Aaron ran to the end, where they encountered the electrified fence.

"Now what?" Aaron asked.

"Don't know," Casper said. "Hadn't thought this far ahead. Thought I was staying behind."

"Put down your weapons," the loudspeaker blasted toward them. "Surrender or be killed where you stand."

Aaron lost what little hope he'd had when he looked over his shoulder. Eight men armed to the teeth flanked a jeep with a military-grade weapon propped up in the back.

"We can't surrender," Casper whispered. "This was a one-way ticket. They get us now, and they'll torture us for days just to watch us squirm. That's not my thing."

"Mine either."

"Then draw their fire."

"What?" Aaron's heart, already beating fast, hit its upper limits.

"I said, draw their fire. Let them shoot at us with everything they've got."

"What? Why?"

"To blow a hole in the fence."

"Or a hole in us."

Casper pulled the pins on his last three grenades.

"Okay," he yelled. "We give up. We surrender." He lobbed a grenade at the base of the fence. Then threw the others toward the jeep.

The only light came from intermittent lamps that ran along the outer fence. Casper and Aaron had stopped at a part in the fence between two overhead lamps. The Jeep's headlights didn't completely reach them. Aaron was sure they were still partly visible to the men standing about eighty yards away.

"Here are your weapons back," Casper shouted. "And your bullets," he said in a lower voice. "Shoot and run to the side. Stay low. Wait for the fence to open."

Casper opened fire as the first grenade exploded at the base of the fence. Two men dropped on the right. Then he dove away from Aaron.

Aaron fired and jumped the other way as return fire showered their area with dirt-eating bullets.

With a history of being shot and left in a wheelchair for months of rehab, Aaron wasn't too keen on being shot again. He stayed down behind a large bush, covered his head with his hands, and waited for the gunfire to stop, but it didn't.

Casper shouted something. Then he was firing. Casper shouted again. Fired again.

Aaron raised his head after an explosion. Casper was on the other side of the fence.

"What are you doing?" Casper shouted. "Let's go."

Aaron saw the hole. The edges still sizzled with electricity.

Casper's grenade.

Casper offered cover fire as Aaron crawled for the hole and rolled through it. Then he got to his feet and headed for open ground, Casper right behind him. They ran and ran, Aaron gaining ground on Casper. It wasn't an age thing, Aaron realized. Casper kept turning around and firing his weapon to deter any followers.

Then his weapon died, and he dropped it in the dirt.

The city glowed in the distance. Aaron could barely make out the straight line of a road on the other side of the reservoir in the dark. He headed that way with Casper jogging beside him now.

At one point, Casper relieved Aaron of his guns and emptied them randomly at any pursuers, but once Aaron had set eyes on the road, he hadn't seen a single person following them.

When they reached the road, exhausted, weakened by the ordeal and adrenaline's retreat, he bent over and gasped for air. Casper was worse off, having not eaten since arriving at the compound.

Without a word to each other, they walked the road toward town, lit in the darkness by a crescent moon, with only a knife each as a weapon. Aaron's severed finger ached, his mouth was dry, and he hadn't known if he would live through the night, but they were free. Somehow they'd done it.

Casper patted him on the back.

"You were something else back there, Aaron. I could use a man like you."

Aaron beamed with pride and kept walking. He couldn't wait to tell Sarah that they'd broken out. It was over. They could go home now. But first, he needed a hospital. Someone had to look at his severed finger to ensure it wasn't infected.

Hospital, then home.

Hospital, then home.

He repeated that to himself as they walked the dark road toward town late into the night.

As the sun rose in the east, Casper found a spot of shelter for a nap fifteen yards off the road behind a thatch of thick bushes. Aaron curled up, the knife under a leaf beside him, and fell asleep almost instantly. He dreamed of a fight scene where he lost the battle and lost Sarah.

When he woke to the bright Mexican sun, his only hope was that his dream wasn't prophetic.

Chapter 28

SARAH HAD CALLED THE police guard into her hospital room and, after a ten-minute debate, got him to agree to allow the group of women to enter for a visit. He would have to record ID and frisk them all, but he agreed.

His biggest issue was that Sarah didn't know the group of women that were coming. She didn't understand why they wanted to see her or how many the group comprised.

Tessa, Sarah's nurse, had just pulled her dinner tray away, and Sarah was adjusting the bed to raise it into a sitting position. The American Embassy had been notified when Sarah had been brought in. The media had discovered that after the assault on the hotel she had been staying with Casper, no one had been able to locate her. To have her show up at the hospital, alive, with broken ribs, had been newsworthy, hence the police guard. The Mexican authorities weren't letting her go until they understood what had happened to her at the hotel and where she had been since.

What was on Sarah's mind wasn't the group of women coming to visit, the newspapers, or the American Embassy. What was bothering Sarah was how long Darwin was taking to arm her with weapons and a GPS location device of some kind before the cartel came for her, which she was sure would happen soon. Darwin hadn't shown up to visit or sent anyone in his place. If the cartel came for her before she contacted Darwin, she would be on her own.

The bed stopped at its peak. She set the remote down and rested her head back.

Vacation.

She needed a vacation and committed to herself and Aaron that she'd take a vacation as soon as this Mexico business was over.

Sarah raised her head at a commotion in the corridor. Was the cartel coming? She heard several women discussing their IDs with the guard through the closed hospital room door.

After a few minutes, the guard knocked.

"Miss Roberts, you have guests."

"Let them in."

The door opened, and the women filed in.

Vivian, what is this about?

"Hello, ladies," Sarah said.

The guard eased the door shut behind them as eight ladies surrounded Sarah's bed. Each one carried a notepad and pen like they were here to take dictation. The women ranged from early twenties to early sixties.

"Allow me to introduce our group," the dark-haired woman on Sarah's left said. "I'm Alexia Purdy, the president of our group, WASP. That stands for Writers, Artists, Specialists, and Perusers. This is my vice president, Sandra Gonzales."

"Seems to me," Sarah said, "I've met you somewhere before, Sandra."

"I was feeling the same thing." Sandra looked at Alexia. "Strange, isn't it?"

Alexia continued the introductions. "This is Debbie Lyons. She writes about her alter ego, Penelope. As a retired teacher, she can portray Penelope in such a way—"

"Can I ask why you've come to see me?" Sarah said.

"Soon. We have to announce each name. It's our WASP sting. Each author and artist needs to be known."

Sarah nodded. "Carry on, then. But don't expect me to remember everyone's name."

A few of the ladies nodded in understanding.

"This is Charlotte Cross. To her left is Lesley Weiler. Then Lavern Skipper and Debra Smith and finally, Lisa Wesley."

"Pleased to meet you all," Sarah said. She studied their faces. "Why do I have the pleasure of your company today?"

"We came to ask you a few questions, if that's possible?" Lavern asked.

One of the women on Sarah's left was hopping from foot to foot.

"Are you okay?"

"Yes, I'm just so excited to meet you."

"Your name was?"

"Charlotte."

"Nice to meet you too, Charlotte."

"I'm Lavern," the woman who spoke a moment ago said.

"We didn't think we'd get inside the room."

"Debra here. The guard said you knew we were coming." She tilted her head sideways and smiled wide. "Is that true?"

"I'm Debbie. Please tell us. Did Vivian give you advance notice?"

Sarah examined their faces, one by one. "You know about my sister?"

"Of course," Sandra jumped in and leaned over the bed. "We've read all of your novels. Some of us have read them twice."

"I'm flattered," Sarah said. "The answer is yes. Vivian told me about you but didn't explain much about your visit."

"We came because …" Alexia cleared her throat. "We wanted to meet you and ask how you survived the hotel ambush. We recently read that El Chapo had escaped from a Mexican prison, setting American and Mexican relations back a decade. Now the Enzo Cartel has its sights on you. The news reported that the Enzo Cartel kidnapped Aaron. Can you verify any of this?"

Most of the women flipped pages in their notebooks and prepared their pens.

What is this, Vivian? An interview?

"Everything you just said is true. Maybe when I'm on vacation in a few weeks, I'll outline the next book on this. I'll call it, *The Cartel*. Do you WASPS approve?"

Two of them giggled. Despite herself, the pain in her ribs, and the nervous anticipation of the cartel coming to the hospital to kidnap her, she was enjoying the WASPS's company. It was fun to talk about books and reading. She only wished she could go to one of their meetings, have coffee and talk longer.

"I'm sorry, it's just so cool to meet you after reading your series," Debra said.

"Thank you, but I really need my rest. What's next for you WASPS?"

Keeping the women any longer than necessary put them at risk. She had met them. They had met her. She did what Vivian had asked for.

"We understand," Sandra said. "We're doing horse research next."

"Horse research?"

"Yes, there's a ranch on the outskirts of Tijuana where we're going to take turns riding horses. Then to the hotel for a few days of writing about our excursion. After that, our two-week WASP vacation in Mexico comes to an end. I'm heading back to Los Angeles. A few of us live in Vegas and other parts of the States."

"How do you have regular meetings if you're so spread apart?"

"Skype and email. And every year, we plan these trips."

"Then thanks for thinking of me, and good luck with your writing."

The women moved away from her bed. Sandra and Alexia remained close.

"We're writing an anthology of short fiction," Alexia said. "Part horror, part thriller. Would you consider reading it when it's done?"

"Of course." Sarah blinked. "Wait, aren't you already published online?"

"I am," Alexia said, her face coloring slightly at being recognized.

"I think I've read one of your ebooks. *Reign of Blood*

series, right?"

Alexia beamed. "That's right."

The door opened, and the guard stepped in. "Visit's over, ladies."

"I loved it," Sarah said as Alexia headed for the door. "And I'll read the anthology. Send me a link when you have the chance."

"We will," Sandra said from across the room.

The door shut, and Sarah was alone again. She dimmed the lights, sipped from her water cup, and shut her eyes to listen for Vivian.

She would rest until Vivian visited or someone else came to her room. When she opened her eyes again, she hoped she saw her savior and not her murderer first.

Chapter 29

A FARMER OFFERED AARON and Casper a ride into town in the back of his pickup truck. They left their knives in the bed of the truck when they jumped out at the hospital. After waving thanks to the farmer, Aaron, and Casper lumbered inside the emergency doors and walked up to the counter.

"We need help," Casper said.

He identified himself and got to a phone where he called in his location. Within ten minutes, two doctors were sent to deal with them, as Aaron had no ID or health insurance card.

When his wound was cleaned and patched up, Aaron met with Casper and headed to the cafeteria for a coffee.

All in all, it took less than two hours at the hospital.

Casper had bought a disposable cell phone and eaten breakfast while the doctors were with Aaron. He told Aaron that he would call in to explain their situation soon. Once they located Sarah, they would all leave Mexico together.

Seated in the cafeteria, the exhaustion of the past few weeks settled over Aaron's system. He needed a home; he needed his own bed. But at what cost? Would the cartel simply show up at his apartment again? Would he have to enter a program like witness protection to stay hidden from them? Give up the life he'd created?

"What's next?" Aaron asked.

Casper pulled his cell phone out. "The cartels have soldiers everywhere. I think it's time to get us out of Mexico."

"Not without Sarah," Aaron said. "As soon as we find her, we can leave."

"Agreed. I'll call in my location and see what updates my office has."

He dialed as Aaron sipped his coffee and looked around the cafeteria.

"Casper," Aaron said in a stern tone. "Put the phone down."

Casper pulled the phone from his ear and set it on the table.

"What is it?" he asked.

"Over there. See those three guys."

Casper turned in his chair. "Yeah. What about them? Wait"—he turned farther—"is that Parkman?"

Aaron got to his feet. "I can't fucking believe this."

Casper got to his feet. "I thought Parkman was in WITSEC," Casper whispered to himself.

Halfway across the cafeteria, Aaron felt the mood by the look on their faces. He saw Daniel, Alex, and Parkman, but no Benjamin.

"What are guys like you doing in a place like this?"

Aaron asked from behind Parkman.

They spun around at the sound of his voice and jumped to their feet in unison, Daniel knocking his chair over.

"Aaron!" Daniel shouted.

Alex clambered around Daniel to hug Aaron.

"Okay, guys, take it easy. What's going on?"

"It's just so great to see you," Parkman said.

"Are your eyes watering, Parkman?" Aaron asked.

"They're not," Parkman said, his tone dropping a notch. "But if they were, I'd appreciate you not outing me like that."

They laughed. They hugged. After a brief moment, Aaron introduced Casper.

"I have him to thank for getting me out of the cartel's compound."

"How's the hand?" Daniel asked.

Aaron looked down at the new white bandages. "Been better. But I'll still be able to run the dojo and teach. Losing one finger won't stop me."

"Where's Sarah?" Alex asked.

"As far as I know, my people are still looking for her," Casper said. He held up the phone. "Waiting for their call back on updates right now."

Parkman frowned. "Wasn't she with you, Casper?"

"She was." He stopped and looked around. "This is the best place. Everyone, take a seat. We need to share information."

As they pulled out chairs, Aaron asked, "Where's Benjamin?"

Daniel and Alex exchanged a look.

"Upstairs," Parkman said. "In surgery."

"Surgery? Why? What happened?"

"He got shot in the shoulder. Doc says it doesn't look too bad."

Aaron reared back. "What have you guys been up to?"

Daniel and Parkman took turns explaining what happened at the border, then how they came to be in possession of the BMW SUV, and how they were going after the cartel to find Aaron.

"That was a close call, guys," Aaron said. "It could've gone either way in that basement. Holy shit. I broke out in a sweat just thinking about you guys down there."

Alex shook his head as he looked at Aaron. "Who knew you'd just walk away from the cartel's compound."

"We didn't quite walk away," Aaron said. "Let me explain."

"Aaron, bring them up to date while I step over here and make another call."

Casper walked away, pressing buttons on his phone.

Aaron explained the last few weeks, starting with the kidnapping. He covered all the torture sessions, including Hector and the helicopter murders and how he jumped into the reservoir. He finished with the bullet ant glove and how Aaron and Casper killed about a dozen men and walked all night until they got a ride to the hospital in a farmer's pickup.

"Whoa, that's quite some story, yourself," Parkman said. "You were as good as dead at any moment. I can't say we were in as much danger."

"Is this a danger competition?" Daniel asked.

They laughed. Some of the tension in Aaron's shoulders eased.

"Now we just need to find out where Sarah is, discharge Benjamin and we can get the hell out of here. Leave the cartel to the DEA."

Casper was coming back, meandering through the tables and chairs scattered about the cafeteria. He seemed happy about something.

"You guys won't believe me when I tell you," Casper said, his eyes watering with excitement.

"What?" Aaron said.

"Yeah, what?" Parkman echoed.

"Sarah was in a car accident."

"And that's good news?" Aaron asked.

"She was riding in a Hummer when she was hit by a dump truck. She sustained cracked ribs."

"A Hummer?" Aaron said. "How the hell did she get a Hummer?"

"She's being treated in a hospital under police guard."

"What hospital—" Aaron started, then stopped and jumped to his feet. His eyes widened in concert with his gaping mouth. "She's here?" he asked, his voice a pitch higher.

Casper nodded. "On the fourth floor. Sarah's being treated right above us. The gang's all here. And she can leave anytime she wants."

Aaron slapped Parkman's shoulder. "Wow!" Then he smacked Casper's arm. "What luck."

"How about we all go up and pay her a visit?" Casper said.

None of them needed to be asked twice.

Chapter 30

A MAN IN A doctor's white lab coat was in Sarah's room, staring at her clipboard. Sarah's half-slitted eyes watched him before they closed again.

"Where's Tessa?" she asked. "My nurse."

"Off shift," he replied.

"You are?"

He set her clipboard down. "Excuse me?"

"Who are you?"

"Dr. Fitzroy." He checked her drip, adjusted something, and looked back at her ribs. "How are you feeling?"

"A little pain. In the side. Nothing else, though. Although … I'm very sleepy."

"You're some kind of hero to make it out of that hotel alive," he said. "Then to stave off an attack by armed cartel members. The media's saying you have a guardian angel."

"You could say that."

Sleepy. More tired than she expected. Her eyes remained closed.

Why can't I open my eyes?

"Well, Sarah Roberts, hitmen and guns didn't kill you. But I will."

Her eyes shot open. She forced them to stay that way as long as she could, but it took incredible effort. He unclipped something under her bed. Then the bed was rolling. Her eyes shut. It was simply too hard to keep them open.

"What's happening?" she asked. "What did you just say? Where are you taking me?"

"You'll be asleep in a moment. When you wake up, you'll be with Enzo. He's waiting for you."

"I don't want to see him."

"It doesn't matter what *you* want."

Her mind drifted. Sleep was coming. He'd drugged her.

"Where's the guard at the door?"

"In our pocket."

"And Darwin. Did he make it here? Please tell me he made it."

"Who is Darwin?"

She listened to the sound of her hospital room door opening. Then she was in the corridor. The guard whispered something. Dr. Fitzroy said something back. She heard *sign here*, then she was being rolled away again.

It was too hard to talk. Her mouth wouldn't move.

The elevator doors opened after a moment. The hospital bed on wheels rolled onto the elevator.

Before the doors closed, she could have sworn she heard Aaron's voice.

Then Parkman's voice. A man shouted something.

Casper? Really? He's still alive?
The elevator doors closed.
Sarah lost consciousness.

Chapter 31

After arguing at the front desk, Casper had to make another call. They got Sarah's room number and ran for the fourth floor ten minutes later.

Aaron was the first one at the guarded door.

The police guard tossed a coffee cup away and gathered his logbook and pens as they approached.

"Is Sarah Roberts in this room?" Aaron asked.

The guard looked up at the assembled men around him. He glanced at all five of them, then shook his head.

"No," he said. "She isn't."

"Where is she?" Parkman asked.

"Transferred to another hospital."

"Bullshit," Casper shouted. "For a few cracked ribs? No way. I want to talk to your supervisor. I want your—"

The guard stepped close to Casper. "The paperwork was correct. I have no say in the matter. She was transferred a few minutes ago."

"Then she's still in the building," Aaron said. "He was just getting ready to leave."

"I'm just the guard," he said, shrugged, and walked away.

Aaron ran for the stairwell, and the rest of the men followed him.

Chapter 32

DARWIN HAD RENTED TWO cars for his mercenaries, who had shown up in Tijuana just as expected. Seven men had come. Others had prior engagements and couldn't make it. Two had been killed in a gunfight in Baghdad. And a few of the others wouldn't get past Mexican customs because of their prior records.

Darwin picked up his men at the prearranged hotel. They had been casing out the hospital for the past few hours. Each man carried two kinds of GPS tracking devices. Each man knew Sarah's safety was the primary goal and that they were dealing with a ruthless cartel. Each man was ready for a little killing. Itching for it, really.

Their primary goal was to track Sarah. Then attack her captors at their location.

They were all identified by the countries they were from. The Greek was called Malaka because he always seemed to be pissed off. The Hungarian was Goulash, and the Russian was called Vodka. There were two Italians, Mario and Luigi. The American was called Bush, but he hated the name. He'd voted for the father but hated the son. And finally, the Canadian. He was called The Beaver, and it had nothing to do with the Canadian national symbol on the five-cent coin and everything to do with his womanizing ways.

Darwin had gone into debt acquiring these men, but Sarah was worth it. He didn't have much to do in Italy but monitor chatter between rival mafia families. So he watched over his close friends, like Sarah. She led an interesting life, and he wanted to do his part to allow her to continue.

Beaver had medical training, so the Canadian did a reasonably good field dressing on his fellow Canadian. The bullet wound in Darwin's arm had recently stopped bleeding, and he was feeling better with mild painkillers. He stayed off the heavy painkillers to keep himself fresh and ready.

Parked outside the hospital's main doors in a communications van, Darwin and Malaka monitored two computers networked through Rosina's system back in Italy. They watched the satellite coverage Rosina had hacked into. The other five mercs had taken up positions around the hospital exits with Vodka on the inside. They watched for people that didn't belong, strange activity, or a chance to see Sarah leaving.

Vodka had radioed in that a commotion had occurred in front of Sarah's door a few minutes ago. Five men had shown up and argued with the police guard. Then the guard walked away.

Sarah was on the move.

"All men in position," Darwin spoke into the mic.

"Goulash."

"Mario."

"Beaver."

"Luigi."

"Vodka here."

He waited for Bush. After thirty seconds, he tapped the mic. "Bush. All okay?"

He waited.

Then, "Bush here" came across the radio.

Darwin exchanged a look with Malaka. "All okay?" he repeated.

"Following the doctor who took Sarah," Bush responded. "He's heading out the south entrance."

"Got him," Vodka said. "I see him."

"GPS that bed or the vehicle," Darwin ordered. "Do not, I repeat, do not let Sarah leave without a locator on her somewhere."

"On it," Vodka replied. "I see Bush now."

Darwin waited. Malaka switched screens to get a better look at the south entrance.

"GPS on the ambulance Sarah was rolled into," Bush reported.

"Good work."

On the computer before him, Darwin brought up the device that Bush had been carrying and entered the code to watch its progress. An indicator popped up on his screen near the hospital's south entrance.

"Malaka, drive this thing. Stay out of sight. I'll guide you as I watch the GPS."

"Yes, sir."

"All units but Bush, make your way back to your

vehicles. Follow the van. Bush, keep an eye on that ambulance until it leaves the hospital."

"10-4."

Darwin sent Rosina a message that they were on the move.

Then the GPS tracker on the ambulance moved on his screen.

"We're rolling," Darwin said into the mic.

Chapter 33

AARON REACHED THE SOUTH entrance as an ambulance rolled away and started for the road. Parkman ran up beside him.

He spun around. "Where's your RV?" Aaron asked, feeling like he was losing Sarah again. He couldn't grasp how this was happening. "Where's that SUV you guys talked about?"

"On the other side of the building," Parkman said. "Three hundred meters off the property." He looked at Aaron. "I'm sorry. We wanted to keep it hidden."

Aaron turned away from Parkman and punched the wall. He placed his forehead on the wall and chanted a soft *no*, over and over. If the cartel had Sarah, he would never see her again. "We just lost her," he whispered. "She's as good as dead."

"Check this guy out," Casper whispered.

Aaron turned to look.

An American was watching them from outside the doors. A large man, the jean jacket he wore far too tight. They stared at each other until he raised a hand to his ear and spoke into a mic.

"He might be cartel," Casper said, a sense of urgency in his voice. "We need to talk to him. He knows something. He's staring at you, Aaron. He recognizes you. He cannot be allowed to leave."

Aaron and Daniel were the first ones out the door.

The man saw them coming. He didn't attempt to flee. He widened his stance and spoke into his mic again.

When Aaron was five feet away, the man produced two guns from under his jacket faster than any magician.

"Ease up, boys," he said.

Definitely American.

Aaron stopped a foot in front of the gun in the man's right hand, Daniel in front of the one in his left. Casper, Parkman, and Alex fanned out behind them.

"My boss wants a word with you five men," the American said. He met Aaron's eyes, looked down at his bandaged hand, then back up to his face. "Are you Aaron Stevens?"

"Who wants to know?" Aaron asked, his tone hard. He opened and closed his one good fist. Then did it again, energy surging through him.

"My boss is Darwin Kostas. He's tracking Sarah as we speak. You want to see Sarah Roberts alive again, y'all want to come with me."

Then the American spoke into his mic, and Aaron decided not to kill him where he stood. He would listen to what they had to say first.

The name Darwin Kostas hit him seconds later.
"Darwin from Italy," he mumbled to himself.
Parkman nodded.

Chapter 34

D ARWIN WATCHED REAL-TIME satellite footage as he studied the GPS tracker. An SUV had pulled in front of the ambulance on the highway and remained there as a guide or added security.

Malaka was two miles behind the ambulance with the mercs piled into two vehicles behind them.

"Hold steady," Darwin said into the mic. "I've got them southbound on Moreno heading out of Tijuana. We're two miles behind. Malaka, pull back even farther. They aren't going anywhere my coverage can't follow."

Malaka eased off.

"Bush here. Got a surprise for you, boss."

Darwin stared at the screen as the two-vehicle convoy eased into the right lane.

"Go ahead."

"I'm still at ground zero and found someone."

The two-vehicle convoy carrying Sarah hit an exit ramp.

Darwin spoke into the mic to Malaka and the rest of the mercs. "Leaving the highway. Stay fresh."

He hit the other mic. "Bush. Busy here. Who did you find?"

"I'm standing in front of Aaron Stevens and a man who calls himself Parkman. They have an American CIA agent with them named Casper and two of Aaron's friends."

Those names struck Darwin like Thor's hammer to the gut.

He looked away from the screen for a brief moment. "Please confirm. Repeat the names. Who do you have with you?"

"Aaron Stevens. Parkman. Casper—"

"Are you sure it's Aaron?" Darwin asked. His heart rate had tripled. "Verify you have Aaron Stevens." What did he do to Sarah by letting her get taken?

"Aaron here." His voice matched what Rosina had recorded years ago when monitoring Sarah's phones.

Darwin looked back at the screen.

"Where's Sarah?" Aaron shouted through the mic. "Have you got her?"

They had missed a turn. Malaka was driving blind with the mercs following Darwin's van. He was supposed to be watching the screen and directing Malaka.

"Abort mission!" he shouted into the mic. "Get Sarah back at all costs. She is not to be transported to the final destination."

"Where do I go?" Malaka responded.

"Where's Sarah?" Aaron was screaming over Malaka's voice.

"Turn right, Malaka. We need to do a U-turn and go back three blocks. They are heading into what looks like a heavily populated area."

Darwin's stomach spun until he felt nauseous. Had he sent Sarah out as bait for the cartel's location in search of Aaron for nothing? When and how did Aaron escape? How would Sarah—and Aaron—ever forgive him? How was he supposed to know Aaron was safe?

Malaka slowed the van as Aaron shouted into the other mic. Darwin watched the two-vehicle convoy on his screen as they entered a residential area, the SUV still leading the ambulance.

He pressed the button to talk. "Aaron, we are going after the vehicles now. We are about to take Sarah back. We need ten minutes of radio silence."

"Ten minutes!" he shouted. "Just tell me where you are. We'll come to you."

"We are headed into a residential area. Give the mic back to Bush, and I'll direct him to our location."

Darwin switched mics. "Malaka, take the next right. We're four miles behind them."

Bush came on the line.

"Bush, switch to our channel."

"Aaron and Parkman have two vehicles," Bush said. "We're heading to them now."

"Go south on the Moreno highway. I'll direct you to our location after that."

"10-4."

Darwin stared at the satellite footage knowing Sarah was inside the ambulance and it was his fault. He hoped she would forgive him as he was only working on the information he'd had at the time.

The SUV disappeared off the screen.

Darwin leaned closer.

The ambulance disappeared.

"What?" he whispered to himself. "How?"

He zoomed the image closer. An overhead bridge. They had parked under it.

"They've stopped driving," he announced.

"Where?" Malaka asked.

"Less than three miles from here. Keep on this road. In two miles, take a right. We will be able to see the bridge they're under at that point."

"10-4."

Darwin waited, tapping his legs nervously, as they raced the two miles. As Malaka turned right, the SUV blasted onto the screen, followed by the ambulance.

"They're on the move again. One mile ahead. Move in. All units move in and retrieve Sarah."

Malaka gunned the van's engine, and Darwin had to hold on to avoid falling off his chair. They were gaining fast. It wouldn't be long now. He verified the GPS tracker. This was their ambulance. Absolutely no doubt about it.

Darwin's van raced under the bridge where the SUV and the ambulance had stopped momentarily.

Bush came on the radio asking for more directions. Darwin offered them. Bush estimated his ETA to be less than six minutes.

"Pulling in front now," Mario said.

Tires screeched outside. The van stopped abruptly. Doors opened, then slammed. Darwin's men shouted orders at the SUV and ambulance.

Darwin tore off his headphones and verified once more that the GPS tracker was on the vehicle outside the van.

It was. They had stopped the ambulance that had taken Sarah out of the hospital.

He grabbed a weapon and hopped out of the van, going slow with the pain in his arm from the bullet wound. The six mercs spread out around the SUV and the ambulance, yelling at the drivers to turn off their engines and get out of the vehicles.

The SUV turned off. Then the ambulance.

The driver's side door cracked open on the ambulance. Darwin was relieved as the driver hopped down and moved away from the vehicle.

They had gotten to Sarah in time. They had saved her. Now he didn't have to face Aaron's wrath. Mario and Luigi subdued the SUV driver quickly. Goulash watched over them.

The ambulance driver began babbling to himself.

"On the ground!" Vodka ordered.

A car raced by. Then another. No one stopped. In fact, they sped up. Darwin figured this much weaponry on the street wasn't new to Tijuana.

He walked to the back of the ambulance and clicked open the door.

"Sarah, Aaron's with us—"

The ambulance was empty.

Sarah wasn't there.

Chapter 35

Whatever Doctor Fitzroy gave her had to be wearing off. Her eyes were lighter and easier to open. Her thoughts wandered, empty. Where was she? What had happened? It was like the past several hours had been erased from her life.

The ceiling above didn't resemble a hospital room ceiling. It resembled wood with evenly spaced squares. The kind of ceiling in a billiards room where men drank glasses of whiskey and smoked cigars.

She looked around the room. Plush, elegant, rich, expensive. This was the home of someone extremely rich. Hunting trophies hung on the walls. Paintings, a chandelier, cherry oak tables.

She sat up to see more of the room but was held back by a strap across her chest and an ache in her cracked ribs.

"What the hell?" Sarah croaked.

Her wrists and ankles were also bound to the table or

gurney they had left her on.

"How many times do I have to be tied up in my life to begin to really hate this game?" she asked out loud.

"You've been tied up before?" a man replied.

She turned to the voice. An attractive man entered the room from behind an abutment in the wall. Late twenties or early thirties. Dressed in a white shirt, black suit jacket, and expensive jewelry. The man looked ready for a photo shoot with GQ.

"What's going on here?" Sarah asked. "Who are you? Where am I?"

"Questions." He shook his head, sat in an overstuffed leather chair in the corner, and examined a fingernail. "Questions are things I use to get what I want. They are not something you are privileged to use."

"What the fuck are you talking about?" Sarah asked, her calm being pushed aside by his maddening demeanor. "I'll ask whatever the hell I want to ask. Are you something with an alphabet? CIA, DEA, FBI, NSA, or one of the other fuck ups who got me in this mess—" She stopped. "You're cartel. You're with the Enzo Cartel."

He continued digging at the fingernail like a demented maniac, worried the nail was cancer he needed to excise.

"You're Enzo, aren't you?"

He released the finger, pulled out a cell phone, and typed on it.

She blew air out between her teeth, turned to stare at the ceiling, and waited. It was obvious they would do it on his terms whether she liked it or not. And she was tied up, so smacking him wasn't an option.

He rose from the chair and slipped the cell phone away.

"I will speak to you soon. For now, sleep."

"I can't sleep. Been sleeping too much. Untie these straps. We'll have a drink over there at the bar and talk. Maybe we'll learn that we have a common interest." She waited a heartbeat, then added. "And I have to pee. I need off this bed thing."

Her head could raise high enough to watch him as he crossed the room. At the door, he stopped, and without turning around, he said, "Sleep."

Then he disappeared. The door closed.

She dropped her head back and ground her teeth.

"Asshole."

The door opened. Her head jerked up. A man in a white lab coat walked toward her.

"You coming to release me?" she asked.

"You could say that," he said.

He had a small box with him. Some kind of kit.

"What's that?"

"A piece of heaven."

"Funny how that works. Today's not the day I go to heaven, so thanks, but no thanks. I don't want your piece of heaven."

"Enzo's orders." He stopped beside her and opened the little box. "You think I'm going to defy Enzo?" He sneered. "Stupid girl."

"Then just tell him you did what you were told—" he strapped something on her arm and started tapping for a vein. "What the fuck are you doing?" she asked, struggling against the tight restraints. She was unable to move her arm more than an inch.

"When I inject you, please refrain from moving. I don't

want to destroy your vein. I don't want to kill you. At least not yet, anyway."

"Inject me?" She surged with panic. "Don't you dare inject me with anything." She glared at him. "Your mistake is fearing Enzo. Inject me, and I'm the one to fear. I will kill you, personally. I'm the enemy here. I'm the one to fear. Remember that."

"Sure, lady," he said. He produced a needle from a table just behind his hip. "Whatever you say."

"What is that shit?" she asked, trying to get a look at the needle. Unless someone broke through the door in a few seconds and rescued her, whatever was in that needle would soon be swimming in her bloodstream. The violation tore at all her core values and beliefs. It drew hatred from dark depths and gave her a determination made of steel to squash men like the one in front of her. She wished for the strength to break her bonds and then his face.

"Heroin," he whispered as he drew close to her inner elbow.

"Heroin!" she shouted. "Do *not* put that in me." The pleading quality of her voice rankled her. "Please, don't." A tear streaked down her cheek. Weakness didn't become her. At this moment, what else was there, though?

The needle broke her skin. It slid in like a deviant alien bug, entering her body to swim unfettered wherever it wanted.

He was talking again, but it was hard to follow. She tried to zone him out and fight the restraints.

"You may experience a shortness of breath, dry mouth, and some disorientation at first," he said. "But it'll ease off until I give you the next needle."

"There won't be a next needle …" Her voice surprised her with its slow lilt. "Stay away … from me."

She shut her eyes and drifted. The blood-restricting strap was removed from her arm at one point, and the pain in her ribs eased off altogether. She actually felt good despite her protests. This wasn't so bad. Maybe these people were nice. Maybe everything would all work out.

She felt like she was walking. Then urinating. Then sleeping. Then nothing.

It will all work out, she thought hours later as the urge for another needle overcame her.

Where's Vivian?

Sarah drifted off to sleep with Vivian nowhere near.

Chapter 36

The RV stopped behind the ambulance, and Aaron jumped out. He ran for the open doors of the ambulance and looked inside.

"Where is she?" He glared at the men surrounding the vehicles. One man with a bandage on his arm stepped closer.

"I'm Darwin Kostas."

"I'm Aaron."

They nodded at each other, each man knowing the other through Sarah but having never met.

"We tracked them here with GPS and satellite coverage," Darwin said.

"What happened then?" He looked around. "I don't see Sarah."

The rest of the men had exited the RV and the BMW and stood behind him.

"We were just learning what happened from those two."

Darwin pointed at two men on their knees, fingers entwined behind their heads. "They stopped under a bridge and took Sarah out of the ambulance while protected from satellite view. They carried her over a ridge and down a small hill to a waiting van, where they left the area. By the time we came upon these two, they were driving empty vehicles."

Aaron stomped a foot and turned to face Parkman.

"Stay calm, Aaron," he said under his breath. "We'll get her back."

"He's right," Darwin said. "We'll get her back."

He spun back around. "How?"

"You are the key."

"Me? How am I the key?"

"They've taken her to where they were holding you. Just tell us where that is, and we'll head on over."

"It's not that easy." Aaron stepped away and stared down the length of the road.

"Why not?"

"Because we walked out at night. Then we hitched a ride into town. I have no idea where we were. Unless Casper here can offer directions, we're fucked."

Casper shook his head. "I can remember a few details, but I don't think I'll be of much use."

"Shit!" Aaron said to himself.

Parkman placed a hand on Aaron's shoulder. "We'll get her back. Aaron, remember, she has Vivian, and she's been in worse situations."

Aaron nodded and lowered his head to stare at the ground.

Behind him, Darwin ordered his men to their vehicles. They needed to clean this up and leave ASAP before the authorities arrived. Two of Darwin's men walked the drivers to their vehicles and tossed one, then the other, in the trunks of the cars. Standing around with this much firepower for more than ten minutes would not get Sarah back alive.

"Aaron, come with us. We'll band together, study maps of the area and try our best to launch a full-scale attack on the Enzo compound." Aaron turned toward Darwin, who continued speaking, "We'll get her back. Trust me."

Aaron nodded. "But first, we must go get Benjamin out of that hospital. We can't leave him there alone. He's unguarded."

"You take one car with two of my men. Once you have Benjamin, my men know where the cabin is."

Aaron nodded again.

Darwin twirled his finger in the air, and his men fired up their engines. Parkman led Aaron toward the RV.

They were rolling down the highway two minutes later, leaving Tijuana behind. Darwin had a place for them to crash, eat, and make plans. A cabin outside the city. A place to regroup.

But Aaron wasn't focused on that at the moment. He needed to get Benjamin safe and then Sarah. Thoughts of Sarah rolled through his mind as he got in the car with Goulash and Bush.

The car pulled away and headed back to the hospital as he closed his eyes and saw Sarah's face in his mind.

How would his life ever be the same without her?

Chapter 37

THE SLAP WAS VIOLENT, shocking her awake with its intensity. She opened her eyes and blinked away the sleep. Her body was heavy, subdued, like her extremities had weight.

The room. Same room. But she was sitting up now. No gurney. No urge to pee. Her clothes had been changed. A gray one-piece, like one found in prison. Everything was so different but still the same.

"Hello," she said out loud.

The slap. Who had slapped her? Where were they?

She looked left, then right. Ice clinked in a glass behind her. She tried to turn but could only go so far. Her wrists prevented the move. She glanced down at them. Duct taped to the armrest.

That's why they're so heavy.

Why? Where am I? Cartel home? She blinked away the mental smoke and thought harder. Why was it so hard to think?

Hospital. Drugged. Gurney in the billiards room.

She looked around again.

This room.

Kidnapped. Drugged.

Heroin.

Heroin. That sweet rush. It wasn't so bad. She eased back in the chair. Comfortable. This wasn't so bad. Why argue if that was all they would do for a few days or weeks? She could deal with it later. She wasn't a druggie. She wouldn't use it once this was over.

Right, Vivian?

She struggled to feel her sister. Nothing.

Vivian?

She closed her eyes and focused on Vivian. Something was wrong. Something kept Vivian from her. Was she disappointed in Sarah? Was she somehow chastising her for thinking the heroin wasn't so bad?

Who are you to judge, sis?

Her face suddenly shot to the right. Someone slapped her again. Harder this time.

"Wake the fuck up!" a man said.

"Hey," Sarah shouted and blinked away the water in her eyes as it rushed over her lids. "I'm up. I'm up."

The good-looking man from earlier moved away and sat across from her on a long plush burgundy sofa, an amber liquid in his glass.

"Holy shit," Sarah said, her face still stinging. "Who are you again?"

"Ask a question." He set his glass down on a large white table that looked like it was made of marble and got to his feet. He maneuvered himself in front of her. "Ask a question —" he slapped her so hard, her cheek resonated with a biting sting—"and get slapped." He retook his seat and picked up his beverage. "I ask the questions, not you."

Sarah glared at him, the pain waking her up all the way.

"You always beat on defenseless women? Is that how you get your rocks off? Oh, wait, that was two more questions, wasn't it? Shit, three." She spit at him, her saliva landing on the white table close to his drink. "Fuck you, pathetic scum."

He offered a half smile, then got up. This time he slapped her twice, once on each side.

"Two for three questions," he murmured and sat back down.

"Overcompensating for the lack of manhood?" she asked.

Now he laughed. But he got up again and slapped her so hard her left cheek went numb, and she tasted blood. The euphoric feeling she experienced upon awakening quickly dispensed.

"Don't sit down," Sarah said. "We're going to be at this a long time."

He remained in front of her. "Is this about control?" he asked. "During this part of our relationship, you own the room? Is that it?"

"Our relationship," she repeated. "I'm not sure what we have is a relationship." She looked up at him, braced for the slap, and said, "Is it?"

He raised his reddened hand. She glared at him and forced a smile.

Then he dropped his hand. "I tire of your antics."

"And I yours."

The man took his seat on the sofa and sipped from his drink. He leaned back, placed an arm along the length of the back of the sofa, and nodded at her.

"You've got guts."

"Untie me. I'll show you what else I have."

"As enticing as that sounds, I don't want you dead yet."

"Why not? I was your goal when you took Aaron. Now you have me. Let's do something about it."

"First, I need to know who those men were."

"What men?" The sting in her cheeks had receded. But now fatigue swept over her. She needed sleep even though she'd slept a lot since she'd been here. Maybe he would give her a taste of that needle again. Just a little one. She didn't want more, but maybe he'd give it anyway. She would never willingly accept drugs when she could do something about it. But as his victim, if he were to …

"The men who followed my vehicles and attempted to break you out. Who are they?"

She examined her bound hands. Then looked at the mark the needle made.

"I was drugged in the hospital." She met his intense eyes. "How am I supposed to know who followed your vehicles?"

"Because you were part of the plan."

"What?"

"My men detected the GPS tracking device instantly. Backup was called in. You were loaded onto another vehicle. The GPS-tracked ambulance was driven away without you in it. But we tracked them. Thirteen men in total. Pulled over and surrounded my vehicles, looking for you. I know a few of them. Parkman, Aaron and Agent Schaffer."

Parkman's here? Casper's alive? But it was the third name that shocked her. *Aaron?*

She focused her eyes on him. "I thought *you* had Aaron."

"I did. Aaron and Schaffer performed a daring escape. They killed several of my men. Good men." He sipped from his drink as if he were talking about men who had simply quit his employ. "I will kill them myself for that. My men deserved better. Aaron and Casper will pay, but that's a matter for another time and has no bearing on our conversation."

The ball in the pit of her stomach got heavier.

"If you had them once," she said. "Chances are unless they come to kill you, they're done here. Casper would call in help and disappear with Aaron."

She realized that Darwin didn't have to let her be taken. Aaron was already on the outside. Why didn't Vivian warn her? Why was she here?

"There were two Canadians from Aaron's dojo," Enzo said, ignoring her comment about Aaron. "I know them. The third one is still in the hospital with a gunshot wound, but he will be dead within the hour."

A bittersweet relief swept over her as she realized everyone had come to Mexico. Everyone was here. But where was Vivian? Which one of Aaron's teachers got shot? How could she warn them that the cartel was heading to the hospital?

"I want to know where the rest of them are hiding," Enzo said. "Tell me who these other men are. The ones who tracked my vehicles. They're professional, organized, and well-armed." He leaned forward on the sofa and placed his elbows on his thighs. "If I'm not mistaken, since I've met men like them before, I would venture a guess they're mercenaries." He eased back, the sofa's material groaning with his bulk. "How the hell have you warranted this kind of help? That's what I want to know. Tell me, why are you so important?"

Her mental faculty cleared even as a mild yearning for another injection rose in her. A steady thrumming of pain developed in her ribcage.

How much of that stuff did they give me?

She understood from what Enzo told her that Darwin had aborted the operation. It all came clear. When she was taken from the hospital, Darwin had been there. He had tracked her as he said he would. Somehow he had discovered Aaron had escaped, and they tried to stop the ambulance he was tracking, but Enzo's men had already discovered they were being followed and switched her to another vehicle.

How did Darwin and Aaron meet?

Couldn't that have happened sooner, dammit?

"I can see you thinking, trying to decide what to tell me," Enzo said. "Don't worry. I will extract every little detail from you."

He pushed a button on his cell phone and sat back, watching her. The wait gave her time to think. If everyone was out there somewhere, looking for her, and Aaron and Casper had just been here—

"Did you hold Aaron here? In this building or on this property?"

"I understand," he said. "Trying to deduce whether or not they can find me again. Maybe even attack me here." He shook his head. "Not a chance. Too heavily guarded. The fence is electrified, and Casper's hole in it has been mended."

"Hole?"

"The one your boyfriend escaped through."

She beamed at the thought of what Aaron did to get out. She was proud of him and happy he had Casper's experience to rely on.

The door opened, and a well-built man in a Hugo Boss suit stepped up to the back of the couch.

"Tell Eduardo to bring the truth serum. Also, more heroin. Once we learn where the cabin is from Sarah, I want her high as a kite until this is over." The man stepped away. "Wait." He stopped and turned back. "Then go to the hospital. Kill Aaron's man, Benjamin. When you're done, call me. I want confirmation Benjamin is dead."

The man checked his watch. "In less than one hour, sir, Benjamin will die."

Chapter 38

Benjamin was just coming out of surgery. Aaron would have to wait, the doctor had said.

Goulash and Bush grabbed magazines in the waiting room and flipped through them while Aaron paced. After twenty minutes, Aaron bought a coffee and continued pacing without thinking to offer one to either of Darwin's men.

The door opened, and Benjamin's doctor emerged, headed down another hallway. Aaron bounded after him.

"Doc, any word?" he asked.

The doctor looked over his shoulder. "Nothing yet. They're transferring him to ICU. He's heavily sedated." The doctor picked up his speed, trying to get away from Aaron.

"When can I see him?" Aaron asked.

This was taking too long. Benjamin wasn't protected here, and Aaron couldn't stand guard while Sarah was in cartel hands. He needed Benjamin safe to devote all his energy to finding Sarah. They needed to get back to the cabin to strategize with Darwin.

"Maybe tomorrow," the doctor said.

Aaron grabbed his arm and spun the doctor around.

"Tomorrow!" he yelled.

The doctor looked down at Aaron's hand, then up and met his eyes.

"Kindly remove your hand."

Aaron did.

"Your friend took a bullet. We operated on him and sedated him. He will pull through this. But now he needs rest. Not visitors. You can see him tomorrow when the police are done with him."

"The police?"

"Yes, it was a gunshot wound. They want to know how it happened. Actually, they will want to talk to you as well. Now, can I go? Can I help other patients, Mr. Stevens?"

Aaron didn't respond. *The police*. He couldn't leave Benjamin here all night. No way.

The doctor walked away, disappeared through a door, and headed down another corridor. Aaron stared at the wall for a moment feeling helpless. He took a deep breath and turned back to the waiting room. Legally he had no grounds to take Benjamin out of the hospital. He wasn't armed and couldn't imagine doing it forcefully.

Unless he convinced Bush and Goulash that was their only option. The cartel's people had just been here when they removed Sarah. If they discovered Benjamin alone in the hospital, he wouldn't make it through the night.

In the waiting room, Aaron sat between Bush and Goulash.

"Guys."

Bush set his magazine down. Goulash just stopped reading but remained holding his.

"Where did you get your names?" Aaron asked. "I can't imagine calling you Goulash. Bush isn't so bad, but …"

"Darwin decided our country of origin would be our names on this job," Goulash said. "But I didn't want to be called Hungary all the time, and Bush here, he didn't want to be called America. Also, we have two guys from Italy. So we fought about it and decided to go with something specific to our country."

Aaron nodded. "Makes sense."

Goulash was one of the biggest mercenaries. He was so wide it was difficult for him to only take up the space one chair allotted. Sitting between Bush and Goulash, Aaron was squeezed in, having to keep his hands on his thighs.

"Okay, guys," he said. "What do we do here?"

Goulash finally set his magazine down now. "What do you mean? We came to get Benjamin and head to the cabin. That's what we do, isn't it?"

"Benjamin just came out of surgery and is in ICU. According to the doctor, we can't get in to see him until the morning."

Bush and Goulash stood in unison.

"Bullshit," Bush said in a deep voice. "He's with us. We take him out now. Hundreds of guys have had gunshot wounds, got patched up, and then went on to fight. He'll be fine."

"They are waiting for the police to talk to him."

"That isn't going to happen," Goulash said. "Where is he?"

"Through that door," Aaron pointed. A man in a black suit opened the door he was pointing at and walked through, closing it behind him. "Where that guy just went."

"We'll be out of here in five minutes, Aaron."

"You guys armed?" Aaron asked.

They both nodded.

"You expecting trouble?" Bush asked.

"I always expect trouble when I'm in Sarah's world."

Bush and Goulash exchanged a glance, then nodded.

"Good policy," Goulash said. "Let's go."

Aaron followed Darwin's men to the door. Once in the next corridor, he asked a nurse where the ICU was, got directions, and the trio headed that way. His stomach filled with anxiety as he considered what they were about to do. He was in a Mexican hospital with two men who were killing machines. They were about to steal Benjamin before he could talk to the police about his gunshot wound. Aaron was a Toronto boy, born and bred, and was only here doing this because he met Sarah. She was a woman with a colorful life. If her life was a palette of paint, she used all the colors, and today's colors were grays and blacks.

But he'd have it no other way. He had never yearned for something, wanted something, and actually ached for something as much as he wanted Sarah. They were all here for her, and each one would take a bullet for her as she would for them.

He clenched and unclenched his fingers, readying himself for what they were about to do, feeling the odd sensation of his missing finger.

The ICU contained multiple rooms. People lay in their beds attached to machines, wires dangling everywhere.

Room after room was full, but none of them contained Benjamin.

At the end of the ICU corridor, the last room on the right was empty except for one bed. The man in the suit they had seen enter the doors by the waiting room before them was standing over that bed, his back to the window. From the angle, Aaron couldn't see the patient's face.

"That has to be Benjamin," Aaron whispered. "Doc said he was in ICU. This is the last room."

A nurse walked by behind them. The man in the suit hadn't moved.

Bush slipped inside the room and waited for Goulash to get in position. Aaron entered and stood beside the door.

The man standing over the bed jerked his shoulders.

"Turn around," Bush said. "Slowly."

Something triggered a response in Bush. He seemed disturbed by the man in the suit.

Goulash moved in quickly and dropped a hand on the man's shoulder.

"My friend here said turn around—"

The man in the suit twisted his upper body and touched Goulash's stomach with something. He raised his hand and twisted it sideways while Goulash's face distorted in shock.

Even before Bush reacted, Aaron understood Goulash had just got stabbed. The world came rushing in as Bush ran past Aaron and slammed into the man in the suit, body-checking him into the wall by the head of the bed.

Aaron took in Benjamin's purple face. The man in the suit had been restricting his airflow. While he tried to take Benjamin's life, he had stabbed Goulash. If they had entered this room seconds later, Benjamin, his friend for over a decade, would be dead.

Bush and the man in the suit were on the floor, rolling left and right in a fight for a gun that Bush held. Goulash had fallen to the side and watched as blood bubbled from his gaping abdomen.

Aaron burst into action. He hopped closer, lifted his right foot, and did an ax kick on the back of the head of the man in the suit. The man dropped like a sack of weights, knocked out cold.

While Bush grunted and eased out from under the other man's bulk, Aaron checked on Benjamin. He was still breathing, but it was labored and fast. His nose was rimmed in red where the man in the suit had held it closed, and the red marks of a hand remained over his mouth.

"Come on," Aaron said. "We're getting him out of here." He got behind the bed and tried to push, but it was secured to the wall.

Bush got to his feet and stood over Goulash.

"Bush, I can't move the bed."

The American stared down at his colleague, ignoring Aaron. Aaron followed his gaze. Goulash's head lagged to the side, his eyes wide and sightless.

"From a stab wound?" Aaron whispered.

"Can you carry your friend?" Bush asked.

Aaron looked at Benjamin sprawled on the hospital bed. He was tall but quite thin. Maybe a hundred and sixty pounds.

"Yeah, I can carry him."

"Then do it and follow me."

Bush turned to the man in the suit, grabbed his hands, and hauled the man up and over his shoulder fireman style. A moment later, Bush produced a small caliber weapon in his free hand.

"Let's go," he said. "What are you waiting for?"

Aaron unhooked Benjamin's IV and heart monitors. Once Benjamin was free of them, a small buzzer sounded on the machine by the bed. He checked the wound to remind himself where it was, walked to the end of the bed, and brought Benjamin along with him.

Not thirty seconds later, he stood behind Bush with his friend draped over his shoulder.

"Go," he said.

Bush led the way out the side exit as two nurses came running down the corridor in response to the buzzer in Benjamin's room.

Understaffed much?

In the corridor, they drew stares. Bush led them to the elevators, where he pushed the button with the tip of his gun and turned to watch the people behind them.

Aaron watched for security, but none materialized.

As the elevator doors opened, he saw a nurse behind her station watching them while talking into a phone.

"She's calling downstairs," he said. "They'll be waiting for us."

"Let them," Bush said as he entered the elevator.

Aaron followed him and pushed the main floor button. The elevator descended fast as Benjamin's weight grew heavier by the second. He began to wonder if he would make it to the parking lot.

The elevator slowed. Bush got into the center, crowding Aaron to the side. They waited. The elevator stopped. The doors opened maddeningly slowly.

No one stood in front of the elevator.

Bush stepped out. Aaron followed.

Two guards lingered to the right. They spoke into their radios, then nodded at Bush.

"No one will stop you," one of the guards said. "You're free to leave the hospital."

Confused, Aaron wasn't about to ask for clarity. He followed Bush outside, ordering his legs to hold the weight of his friend. They made it to the car and stopped. Bush set his unconscious man on the pavement.

"Shit," he said.

"What?" Aaron asked as he laid Benjamin down on the trunk. He rolled his shoulders to loosen them. "What's up?"

"Goulash has the keys."

"Oh shit, you serious?"

"Afraid so."

"Dammit."

Aaron glanced around the parking lot. Then dropped to the man in the suit and rummaged through his pockets. He came out with a set of car keys.

"Let's use his car," he said as he pushed the button on the key fob.

Seven cars over, a newer model BMW's lights blinked. He pushed it again.

"Let's go," Aaron said.

He hauled Benjamin back over his shoulder and made it to the BMW without trouble. He laid Benjamin down in the back seat, squeezed his legs in to fit, and then closed the door.

"The trunk," Bush said.

Aaron popped the trunk as the man in the suit was

coming to. He moaned, flailed his arms a little, and tried to speak. Bush hefted him off his shoulder, twisted, and dropped the man into the trunk, banging his head on the way in.

"Ouch," the man said. "That fucking hurt."

"You have no idea the pain you're in for," Bush said before he slammed the trunk. Then he slapped Aaron's arm. "Good work. Let's go."

On the way out of the parking lot, the two guards stood watching their progress.

One of them nodded as if they knew each other.

"Paid off," Bush said from the passenger seat.

"Paid off?"

"The guy in the trunk was hired to kill your friend. He's a hitman." Bush flipped through the stations on the radio while he talked. "The cartel paid big bucks to have him gain access to Benjamin. The doctor knows. The nurses know. And those two guards know." He stopped on a station playing Led Zeppelin. "That's why they gave us a free pass. They think we're cartel men."

"I want to go back and shoot them for that."

"Don't worry. You'll get your chance."

Bush moved his head to the beat of "Whole Lotta Love" as it blasted from the car speakers.

Chapter 39

IT TOOK AN HOUR until the man named Eduardo returned with a small briefcase. She remembered him from earlier. He had given her relief and comfort. The pain had disappeared. But she didn't want more drugs. Just something for the pain.

Enzo got up, took his empty glass to a cabinet, and filled it while Eduardo sat beside Sarah and set up his equipment.

"Tell me about your sister," Enzo said a moment later.

She had been paying attention to what Eduardo was doing and gapped. Somehow Enzo had walked back over to stand on the other side of her.

"Fuck you."

"Interesting answer." He moved to the sofa and sat in the corner, twirling his glass in a circle. "What happened to Vivian?" He met her eyes. "Come on, Sarah. You can talk about family, can't you?"

Eduardo wrapped her arm above her elbow and prepared

a needle. She flexed her arms and legs to test the bindings, but nothing gave way. Even the restraint around her chest held solidly. She grunted and let a wheezing sound out through her nose.

The war was on the inside. Rationally, she wanted nothing to do with drugs. But irrationally, the euphoric feeling she experienced earlier waited on the other side of that needle.

"I'll know everything as soon as what's in that needle starts to work on you."

Sarah jerked her head back and tried to knock over the chair, but it didn't budge more than an inch. Eduardo wrapped a firm hand over her forearm and, without missing a beat, eased the needle into Sarah's arm. She felt the needle's release enter her bloodstream and turned to glare at Eduardo.

"That is the last time you do that to me."

Feeling hopeless, losing freedom, and being tied down and secured made her feel weak. No matter how much she thrashed, there was no moving, no getting out of the chair. She was subject to the will of another human being completely. The man wanted her dead. He was definitely the kind of man who played with his toys before he killed them.

She glowered at Enzo as her mind was lost to her. He offered a warm smile in response.

Vivian. Why?

Her sister remained silent.

"Are we finished, Eduardo?"

"Yes, sir."

The man beside her packed up. Sarah rolled her head from him to Enzo and back. The pain in her ribs subsided again, and she couldn't hold herself up too well.

She giggled. "Good thing I'm in a chair. Like this," she said. "You know. Or I'd fall."

Something was wrong with her speech. She couldn't figure it out. Unless she thought about it hard enough. Maybe.

"What does Vivian do?" Enzo asked.

Elated to hear Vivian's name, Sarah smiled and let her heavy head rest downward.

"She talks to me. She's so special."

"What does she talk about?"

"Oh, you know. Things."

"Explain these things."

"Bad things." Her voice turned stoic. "Harsh things. She tells me about bad men like you, and then I kill 'em." She giggled and wondered why she had the urge to giggle when they were being serious.

"You kill bad men?"

She tried to remain serious. "As often as I can."

"Do you want to kill me?"

She nodded, bobbing her head up and down so hard she saw stars, then tried to focus on him.

He looked at the watch on his wrist. Sarah noticed a tattoo by the watch for the first time.

"You have an hour or so left."

"For what?" she asked. "A car ride? Lunch? A nap? Tell me. What happens in an hour?"

Eduardo finished packing up his briefcase and headed for the door.

"Bye-bye, dickhead," she said.

He didn't look back.

Enzo snapped his fingers to get her attention. "In one

hour, you will cease to exist. I am going to kill you in one hour, Sarah. Then you will be with your sister. Would you like that?"

"I would like to see my sister. Yes. But," she shook her head, "I don't want to die to do it. Not yet, anyway. Pretty sure about that."

"Where do the mercenaries stay while in Tijuana?" Enzo asked.

"A cabin." She said it before she could stop herself. What did it matter? He couldn't find one cabin in all of Mexico.

"Where is this cabin?"

"Somewhere in Mexico," she said, then laughed. It felt so good to laugh.

"Be more specific."

"An hour from here. Maybe less." There's no way he could find it. No way. She added, "Nice place, too. Comfortable."

"A nice breeze?" he asked.

Nothing about its location. Good.

"Yes, each afternoon. A salty breeze. Sit out on the deck, you know."

"I do know."

He lifted his cell phone and spoke into it. "You got that?" he asked.

A man on speaker phone replied. "Roger that."

It sounded like he was in a car on the road, window down.

"Within a forty-five-minute drive of Tijuana, near the water. A cabin. Check the ones recently rented out. Study satellite images. It'll be secluded enough that neighbors can't see much. It narrows it down to probably a dozen buildings or less."

"Roger that. The research should take thirty minutes. Our team is assembled. My guess is we locate the cabin and launch an attack within one to two hours."

"Make it faster."

"On it."

Enzo set his phone down.

"What are you doing?" Sarah asked. Her eyes were so heavy; she kept them shut now. It was too difficult to fight them anymore.

"Killing everyone you know today. I have patience. I'll wait until your parents are released from hiding. I'll get them later."

A violent paranoia surged through her. She started to cry. Her bottom lip quivered.

What did they give me?

"You can't do that," she said.

"I am doing it."

The phone rang as she cried harder and began chanting the word *no* over and over.

"Speak," Enzo said into the phone.

"Your men are clear of the hospital."

"You will be rewarded handsomely."

"Thank you. Just thought you should know."

"Send my regards to the missus—wait." Enzo stared at the ceiling. Sarah had opened her moist eyes and watched his face.

"Sir?"

"You said, *men.*"

"Yes, sir. Two men entered the hospital and took the patient Benjamin out. A man tried to stop them. He was stabbed and left behind. They drove away in the BMW you said your men were driving." The man on the speakerphone cleared his throat. "Did I do something wrong, sir?"

"I sent one man in a BMW. He wore a dark Hugo Boss suit. Is this the dead man left behind?"

Enzo's knuckles grew white with strain as he squeezed the cell phone waiting for an answer.

"No. The man left behind is a very large UFC fighter or something. He was stabbed so badly in the abdomen that he died within a few minutes."

"That sounds like my man's work."

"I saw the man in the Boss suit."

"Where?" Enzo asked.

"He was carried out and placed in the trunk of a BMW."

Enzo lifted the phone and got ready to throw it across the room but stopped and yelled into it, snapping Sarah fully awake.

"What did the men look like?" he shouted.

"Who?"

"The ones in the Beemer."

As Sarah listened and tried to stay focused, she heard the caller describe Aaron and another man.

Enzo slowly turned to Sarah. Then he did throw the phone. It bounced off her cheek and smacked into the wall a few feet beside her.

"Ohhh," she moaned as blood dripped into her mouth.

"I will skin you and Aaron alive. I will pull out your eyes." Enzo jumped off the sofa and ran at her. She opened her eyes wide to take him in as he rushed at her. She stopped breathing in fear and anticipation. What was happening? Who was this guy? How did she come to be here?

He grabbed her hair and yanked her head back, then screamed into her face, his saliva mixing with her blood as it ran off her face.

"You will die. You will feel pain. You are going to scream for hours before you pass out, then I'll wake you the fuck up to die again. Do you hear me?"

Out of nowhere, Enzo's knee rose and connected with the side of her head. The chair tipped over. Before it hit the carpeted floor, Sarah lost consciousness.

Chapter 40

Bush pulled up to the cabin and parked. Together they worked on getting Benjamin out of the back seat. During the ride, he had remained sedated by all the drugs they'd given him.

Darwin came out to help without asking where Goulash was. Once Benjamin was lying on the ground, Parkman and Alex carried him inside.

"We lost Goulash," Aaron said.

Darwin gestured at the cabin. "Explain inside so everyone can hear."

Once inside the cabin, Aaron and Bush explained what happened at the hospital, how they got to Benjamin just in time, and how the doctor and hospital security had to have been paid off. Everyone listened as they explained, leaving the keys in Goulash's pants. But the guy in the trunk had keys to the Beemer.

"The guy in the trunk?" Darwin asked.

"Right," Aaron said, looking at Bush.

"Hadn't gotten to that point," Bush said. "Thought we'd bring him along to tell us where the Enzo Cartel hides out."

"Well then, let's get started," Parkman said.

The team headed outside to the Beemer. Forming a semi-circle around the trunk, with the Italians, Mario and Luigi, their guns ready, Bush popped the lid with the key fob.

The hitman in the Hugo Boss suit covered his eyes from the bright sunlight. Darwin and Bush hauled him out of the trunk and dropped him on the gravel.

"He tried to kill Benjamin," Darwin said. "We're going to have fun with this guy." He gestured at Malaka and Beaver. "Get him inside. Mario, Luigi, if he does anything stupid, just shoot him."

"Yes, sir. Pleasure."

They dragged him inside by his feet. He twisted and tried to roll up in an attempt to get his shoulder blades away from the ground but couldn't. Only faint grunts escaped his lips when they bumped him over the two stairs before the open door.

"We're running out of time," Darwin said. "We need to know what this guy knows and fast. Sarah's life depends on it."

"I've done interrogations in Iraq," Malaka said. "I can handle it."

"I don't want him killed, though," Darwin added. "He can die later. Information first."

"Can't guarantee anything," Malaka said. "To make him talk, well, let's just say, it can get brutal."

Darwin exchanged a look with Parkman.

"Make him talk at all costs," Parkman said. "That's my opinion."

"Agreed," Darwin said. "Enzo compound location is our primary goal. We leave within an hour."

"Got it." Malaka half ran for the cabin.

Clouds rolled in. It would rain soon. A breeze had picked up as Aaron listened to the exchange between the men and began to zone out. More death and torture. Why did Sarah's life have to be so complicated? Would they locate her in time? Was she already dead? He was still outside when the rain started falling. He was still outside when everyone else had gone inside.

Aaron was still outside when he heard the man in the suit screaming and begging for Malaka to stop.

Aaron let the water soak and cleanse him, leaving him dirty for it. He would never be clean again.

Then there was more screaming from inside the cabin.

Chapter 41

SARAH FELT THE WATER splash across her face, gasped, sucked in the sweet air, and woke up. The buzz from the drugs was wearing off. She was awake. A strong urge from her bladder and a dry mouth confused her momentarily. Hunger made noises inside her abdomen.

Why was water splashed on her face?

A red bucket was cast aside by her feet. She scanned the room. Enzo leaned against a wall, tapping furiously into his cell phone.

"Good," he yelled at her. "You're awake."

"Hey, thanks. You could've just tapped my shoulder."

Enzo had the harried appearance of someone frazzled. His hair was askew, jacket gone, and shirt unbuttoned. His actions were frantic and seemed rushed.

His cell phone emitted the tinny sound of a ring.

"You can put that thing to your ear, you know."

He looked at her with red-rimmed eyes and shook his head. "Cancer. I don't want this cell field," he rolled a hand around the phone, "giving me cancer by getting too close to my head. No fucking way."

"*Hello?*" someone said through the cell phone's speakers.

"They have the BMW," Enzo shouted.

"*So?*"

"What do you mean, so? Are you thick? Trace the fucking car. Track it. You've done it before. Wherever the BMW is parked, you will find the men who took him."

"*Oh, yeah, right. Good thinking. I'll do it now.*"

Enzo jabbed at the phone and slipped it into his back pocket. He pushed off the wall and started toward her. "I wanted you awake. Within minutes, my men will kill everyone at the cabin." He held the phone in the air and shook it. "I want you to hear Aaron scream before he dies. When that's done, I will kill you softly for the rest of the day. No more drugs. No more playing. Just death." He smirked. "You didn't have any other plans for the day, did you? I'm not interrupting your busy schedule of attacking and murdering bad guys, am I?"

Sarah tightened her hands into fists and lifted upward, but the duct tape held firm. She met his steely gaze and knew if the odds were evened, she would beat him in a fight. For him to win, she had to be subdued, tied down.

"I have no regrets. Yet I still think I'm the one who will walk away from this, not you." When she talked, she felt soreness and mild swelling where he had kneed her in the cheekbone earlier.

"How's that?" he asked.

"It's just the way it is."

"Cocky bitch, eh? Tell me, why do you have no regrets? Look at you now. You don't regret being in this helpless condition?"

"I'm not completely helpless." She thought about her answer more. "The biggest regret people have on their deathbed is that they tried to live the life expected of them, not the life that was true to themselves. I've been true to myself. At least since I turned eighteen. So, yeah, no regrets." She shook her head to flick hair out of her eyes. "How about you? Anything you'd change since you'll be dead before the sun goes down?"

Enzo laughed hard and loud. At one point, he slapped his leg. Only the sound of his phone ringing stopped him.

He pulled it out and smacked the front of it.

"Speak," he said, a bit of the laughter still evident.

"Located the cabin on GPS. Fifteen minutes out."

"Good. Call me when you have Aaron. Kill him on the phone. I want this bitch to hear it."

Sarah tugged at her restraints again but to no avail.

"Sir, we will be leaving evidence behind. We need to get in and get out. I'll need cleansing on this one."

"Done. I'll have the helicopter filled with the necessary explosives and brought to your location within an hour."

"Thank you, sir."

Enzo hung up and dialed someone else while Sarah scanned the room again, looking for anything she could use to break the duct tape. At this point, she would toss her hands into a fire to burn the tape off if it meant escaping the chair.

Someone picked up on the other end of Enzo's phone. "Fill the chopper with enough explosives to clear a house,"

Enzo said into the phone. "You've got forty-five minutes. Be in the chopper and ready to fly as soon as possible."

He hung up as Sarah struggled against her bindings.

"You won't break that tape," he said. "Why try?"

"Because the urge to kill you has become overwhelming."

"Stand in line. You have no idea how many people want me dead."

"How's that for your self-image?" she asked.

He got up from the couch, walked to the front door, and grabbed an umbrella. The rain pounded on the roof and front door behind him.

Then he strode back across the room, lifted the umbrella like a baseball bat, and swung at Sarah. It stung, and with each consecutive smack, it stung harder. He didn't stop whacking her with it until the umbrella had broken in half and was useless.

"An hour left," he said, gasping for air. "One hour left, and you start to die."

"From the moment I was born, I was dying. Today is no different."

Chapter 42

MALAKA STEPPED OUT OF the back bedroom of the cabin and closed the door. His hands and several parts of his body were covered in blood.

"I wouldn't go in there," he said in his strong Greek accent. "Not a good scene."

Darwin got up from the table and left his coffee cup behind. "What did you learn?" he asked. "Tell me you got something out of him."

Malaka shook his head. "Nothing. He wouldn't give Enzo's place up. Said Enzo would do worse to him than anything I could dream up." Malaka shrugged. "Guess I went a little too far. His heart gave out when I was grinding my screwdriver along his calf bone. Sometimes when you puncture the skin and twist the screwdriver into the shin, they get pretty fucked up when it touches the bone. Never had one die on me, though. Dammit, man. Sorry, Darwin."

Darwin patted him on the shoulder, then turned around. He looked into the eyes of every man there, one by one. The weight on his shoulders of letting Sarah get taken was suddenly heavier.

"There has to be something," he said. "Aaron, Casper, can you remember anything about the walk away from the compound? What about you, Aaron? You spent a few weeks there. What did the house look like? Incoming roads? Fences? Would it be something you'd recognize from satellite photos?"

"Wouldn't hurt to bring in a computer, and I'll start looking at properties within an hour's drive of Tijuana. Something somewhat secluded." He snapped his fingers. "It had a reservoir. That will narrow the search down. Wish we had that GPS tracker, though. That would lead us right to Sarah."

Bush jumped to his feet like he'd been electrocuted.

"What is it?" Darwin asked.

Bush glared at him like he was angry for a moment. "I can't believe I didn't think of it before."

"What?" Darwin asked.

"Yeah, what?" Aaron added.

"GPS. There's one in the BMW." He pointed at the room Malaka had just exited. "That dead asshole used GPS. The Enzo compound might be in the GPS's history."

Darwin turned and bolted for the door. He smashed it open and ran for the car with feet pounding behind him to catch up. The first one to the car, Darwin turned the GPS on and instantly accessed its history. A list of addresses popped up on the screen. He scrolled down, studying them. One remained common.

"Get the computer," he yelled to no one in particular. "Aaron, Casper, stay with me."

While he waited, Darwin ran through the rest of the history and determined the address he suspected was either the hitman's home or the Enzo compound. For all he knew, that could be one and the same.

Malaka shoved the computer through to Darwin. He brought up Google Maps and typed in the address, then dropped the little man down for street view and handed the computer to Aaron.

"This it?" Darwin asked.

Aaron nodded furiously. "Yes, that's it!"

They had found the compound in less than a minute.

"We've wasted enough time. Everyone," he shouted at full volume now. "Mount up. Grab everything and be ready to go in less than five minutes. Go! Beaver, stay with me."

The men scattered. Darwin had enough Kevlar vests for everyone and enough guns for each man to carry two. What he needed was for a man to stay behind and clean up. Once they had Sarah, they wouldn't be coming back here.

"Beaver, bury the driver of this BMW out back in the woods. Then take an hour to clean the place. Walk to the highway and wait for my call. When we're clear of the compound, we'll come to pick you up."

"Consider it done, eh," he said and smiled.

"Okay, eh," Darwin mimicked and headed inside to grab his gear.

Today was their last battle in Mexico. He not only hoped he would get Sarah free of this cartel, but he also hoped he could get back to pick up Beaver. He'd hate to leave a fellow Canadian behind.

It wasn't just that. He didn't want to lose another mercenary on this trip. But something told him, deep down, that he wouldn't see Beaver ever again.

Chapter 43

Enzo had calmed down. He'd ordered all his men but five to leave the compound and head to the cabin where Darwin was hiding out with however many men he had. Frustration and helplessness overwhelmed Sarah. With Vivian gone, an internal conflict raged inside her. A battle with Vivian went one-sided as Vivian still remained quiet. It had to mean Sarah would be fine, that Sarah was on the right path. Otherwise, Vivian would step in and change things.

But how could this be the right path? Darwin, Parkman, Daniel, and all the other men at the cabin were about to be slaughtered while Sarah fought the urge for another needle.

The homicidal maniac pacing the floor in front of her caused a hatred she'd never known before. She would fight and subdue, and sometimes, if needed, Sarah killed people. Enzo made her yearn to kill him. No fight needed. Nothing else. Just death. Then this would all be over, and they would be free. The search for the black book in Amsterdam and Greece. The fighting in Europe, and the fighting in Toronto, had led to this moment. She wouldn't change a thing but suspected Vivian could've changed a lot of things along the way.

Yet hope was an elusive bitch. Hope made her believe that ultimately she was at the right place at the right time, and everything would work out. Unless, of course, she was supposed to die. That was the one thing she could never count on. When that happened, it would just happen, and chances are she wouldn't even know until she was dead.

Enzo's phone rang. He clicked a button.

"Speak."

Sarah glared at him, heat oozing off her face.

"We're onsite and approaching the cabin from the rear," the caller said.

"Do you have absolute certainty this is the right place?" Enzo asked with a quick glance at Sarah.

"Yes, sir. One man is dead. We caught him with a shovel fifty yards behind the cabin. He had just started digging a hole."

"For what?" Enzo turned to face Sarah.

"He was burying a man in a nice suit. A Hugo. He was tortured, sir. The man with the shovel was burying what remained of the body."

Enzo's jaw tightened. He stared back at Sarah.

"Kill them all," Enzo said. "The helicopter will be ready in minutes. It's loaded with enough bombs to level the cabin. Just fueling it now. Give precise directions when you've executed everyone. And call me when you have Aaron."

"Will do."

Enzo clicked the phone off. He moved to stand in front of Sarah.

"This is it," he said. "The end of your life begins now."

He produced a needle from somewhere behind him and jabbed it forcefully into her arm, plunging the top all in one motion.

She fought, she struggled, but it was no use. Her limited movement constricted her to only shaking. The drug took effect almost immediately, and a sense of peace eased over her. The pain in her cheek from his knee and the cracked ribs eased off.

"What'd ya go and do that for?" she asked.

He ripped the duct tape off her chest, then tore it from her wrists.

"Just enough to get you high but still responsive. You have to walk on your own, and I don't want to fight you."

She giggled. Then frowned. "Fight? Why fight? You win."

"That's better."

He snapped the duct tape off her ankles and dragged her to her feet. Having sat for so long, her legs were weak. The intense pressure in her bladder also eased off as Enzo walked her toward the door. She tried to swing at him, but the feeble attempt only tapped his arm.

"You'll enjoy my barn, Sarah."

She thought he was joking about something. "Sounds good to me."

"I'm interested to know. How does death make you feel?" he asked. "You've been communicating with the dead for some time, and now you'll be dead. Any last thoughts?"

"Nope. None. But I'm not going to die."

Someone shouted by the front gates. Enzo stopped guiding her. Sarah stared at several ladies she had seen before but couldn't remember where.

"What the fuck is this?" Enzo asked no one in particular.

At the gate, a group of women were arguing with security. From their loud voices and the lack of interfering noise, Sarah gathered that these women were supposed to be given a tour of the grounds and then a two-hour horse ride. They demanded to know why it was being canceled.

Sarah recognized Sandra Gonzales, who turned toward Sarah and pointed. They had said something about riding horses before they flew back to the States. Then she saw the familiar face of Alexia Purdy. The WASPS had come to save her life as Vivian had predicted.

"That's Sarah Roberts," Sandra yelled. "She's been missing from the hospital. We demand to know what you're doing with her here."

"Yeah," Alexia joined in. "I think we need to call the police."

Enzo spun Sarah around and headed back to the main house. Once inside, he tossed her forward, where she fell to the carpet. By the time she rolled over, Enzo had his phone out, and it was already ringing.

He clicked something on it and shouted, "Get rid of them."

"I'm trying, sir."

"Try harder."

"They have tickets for the horses. They're demanding entry—"

"Either kill them all or remove them from the property. Or kill yourself, and I'll come to do it because what would I need you for if I have to come and do your job? You've got one minute."

He turned and punched the wall two-handed.

"Problems?" Sarah asked, then giggled.

"I hide in plain sight," he said without looking at her. "We offer daily horse rides."

"Horse rides." She sniggered. "A cartel that sells cocaine and offers horse rides. Oh man, that's funny. You're a riot."

"This house is a charity organization. No one would know what really goes on here. And no one will ever know."

His phone rang.

"What?"

"They're gone. But they saw Sarah."

"Fuck!"

"They're coming back." He paused on the line. "Possibly."

Enzo clicked off. He ran at Sarah, grabbed her arm, and hauled her back to her feet.

His phone rang again. He let her go, and she crumpled to the floor.

"What?" he shouted.

"Cabin's empty, sir."

"It's what?"

"Empty. No one is here. They're gone. The Beemer's gone."

Enzo turned in a complete circle on the carpet. "I thought you said this was the place."

"It is. But no one's home."

"Where might they be?" Enzo asked. "Did you ask the guy with the shovel before you killed him?"

"No, sir."

Enzo threw his phone across the room, panting like he'd run a few miles. His face flamed red, and his eyes swelled.

"This is all because of you. Those women will come back with the authorities. I'll have more people to pay off. I've lost millions of dollars because of you. Over a dozen men were killed when Aaron and that American agent escaped. All because of you."

"Pick your opponents more wisely," Sarah said, trying to maintain a straight face while enjoying the shit out of this moment.

"The way to solve all this is to have you dead. I have to have you dead as soon as possible."

He grabbed her arm and lifted her up. Dragged behind him, Enzo rushed her back out the door and barely missed being killed by the volley of bullets that raced by in front of him.

Enzo ducked and jumped back inside the house even as the glass in the windows broke inward from the fusillade.

Chapter 44

ON THE RIDE OVER, following the BMW's GPS, Darwin outfitted everyone with an earpiece. Parkman drove the RV until they got to the access road that led to the address. No other houses were in sight, and the trees were the same as Aaron and Casper remembered.

After hiding the RV under tall trees, Darwin eased the Beemer along the access road while the men ran behind it.

When the guard tower came into view, the men dispersed into the trees and made themselves scarce. Darwin edged the BMW along the driveway with Malaka, the only one staying behind it, bent over, hidden by the trunk.

The guard tower door opened—the rain must've obscured his view through the shack's windows—and the armed guard stepped out.

Malaka rose up, aimed, and took the shot.

The guard jerked back and fell on the wet pavement.

Darwin waited. Malaka waited. No other guard stepped out.

Darwin started forward again. At the gate, he pushed the garage door opener button on the sun visor, and the gate slid open.

The rest of the men emerged from the trees on either side of the BMW, and as a unit, they entered the grounds without resistance.

The moment they did, Darwin saw the door open on the side of the large house in front of them. A tall, well-dressed man exited with Sarah in tow. The relief at seeing her alive stunned him into temporary paralysis.

It was Malaka and Bush who began laying bullets down in front of the man, hoping he'd panic, drop Sarah's hand and become exposed, or simply leave her there and run. He did just that but dove for cover back inside the house.

Seconds later, they scattered at the return fire. Darwin dropped sideways along the front seat of the BMW as the windshield shattered inward. When there was a break in shooting, he scooted sideways, dropped onto the grass from the passenger door, and rolled behind the car as another volley of bullets rammed the front.

"I'll cover you," Malaka shouted.

Darwin watched and waited. Then Malaka stood, shouldered his AR-15, and let loose.

Scrunched down, Darwin ran for cover behind the guard shack at the gate.

As far as he could tell, none of his team had been hit yet.

Then the BMW exploded, knocking Malaka off his feet even though he was ten yards from it.

Darwin covered his ears and screamed.

Chapter 45

SARAH CRAWLED TOWARD THE open door as bullets rocketed all over the grounds. Bullets hit brick, glass, and stone, making soft punches as they bit into the earth.

It seemed like an eternity before she could reach the safety of the house, the whole time wondering who was shooting.

At the open door, she crawled in and rolled away for cover. Her arm caught under her ribs, and she screamed at the pain. She instantly rolled again to get off her wounded side and grunted.

The gunfire outside didn't abate. Glass broke somewhere close by. She jerked as something exploded outside. Her drug-addled mind tried to focus. She tried to stand but fell on her butt. Why wouldn't her legs work? They felt rubbery. She tried again, got to her feet, and staggered as her vision slanted the room, first to the right, then left.

What had Enzo given her?

She made it to the open door and looked up. There were five different places along the roof where the barrels of guns lined the edge. One would disappear while the others fired. Then another would disappear only to be replaced by two more. Enzo's men were firing back. Whoever they were attacking by the road was losing.

She crept low to the front window that had been blown out. She tried to see who was out by the front gate but couldn't as they were well hidden. Whoever they were, approaching in a BMW—such a nice car—wasn't probably the best idea.

A beefy hand wrapped around her arm and shoved her through the open window. She smacked into the ground and rolled onto her back. The rain pattered down on her face. She tried to blink it away, but it was relentless. Her inflamed ribs screamed.

Before she could try to get up, a man lifted her toward the helipad, where the chopper was already spinning its rotors. Another man beckoned them from behind the front bubble of the machine that, for some odd reason, made her think of a housefly's eyes.

She laughed despite the pain as Enzo—she knew it was him carrying her now—with a rabid dog's determination on his face, ran for the chopper. With every step, she tried to get her feet under her, but it was no use. He held her tight, like a doll under his arms.

The world spun. Dizziness set in to the point where it appeared the chopper was already flying in a strong wind.

Someone called her name. A volley of weapon fire answered the shout.

She heard her name again as they reached the chopper and could've sworn it was Aaron's voice.

But they're all dead. Aren't they?

She sprawled on the floor of the chopper as it lifted off. She slid and bumped into the seats at the front as the chopper's nose dipped. A wall of boxes with hazardous materials markings were strapped in at the back of the chopper. Enzo had talked about filling the chopper with enough bombs to raze Darwin's cabin.

Is that where we're headed now?

A quick look out the side of the helicopter revealed the roof of the house as they passed it at an angle. A total of five men dressed in black continued to shoot toward the front gate and the flaming BMW just inside the entrance.

Then something happened to her hand.

It numbed.

Vivian?

Her arm numbed. Her chest numbed. And Vivian swooped in like a long-lost friend. The narcotic's effect disappeared as Vivian took control.

Finally.

Sarah got to her feet and grabbed a safety strap dangling from the chopper's side as it rose into the sky. She swung out and around and delivered a sidekick to the pilot's head, snapping his helmet off as it bounced off the window. She landed on her feet, leaned between the two front seats, and elbowed Enzo so hard blood spurted from his nose. She jabbed at his throat as the pilot turned to see who hit him. Sarah felt in control yet, at the same time, a puppet. Vivian offered a retreat from the drugs momentarily. The fighting was all Sarah.

The pilot let go of the control stick to clutch at his throat. Enzo recovered faster. He lunged from his seat as the machine hovered and wobbled in the air. He landed on her in an awkward position and flailed at her. Sarah took the blows one by one as she squirmed under him.

After five blows, with blood seeping out of a cut to the forehead, Sarah drove her knee into Enzo's crotch. He lost the will to fight as he curled into a ball and rolled off her. She grabbed the gun from his waistband and rolled the other way.

The open door came quickly, and she had to grab the safety strap to stay inside the chopper.

The pilot had regained the stick. She caught the look in his eyes as he swung the machine to the left, tossing her about.

The next moment Sarah was airborne. If it weren't for the solid grip on the safety strap, she would've fallen a few hundred feet back to the ground.

Dangling outside the chopper, Enzo's gun in her free hand, she aimed and fired twice at the pilot's head.

The machine righted, and Sarah was flung inside, where she smacked into Enzo, who was clinging to the mesh that held the explosives inside. In a brief flash, Vivian still controlling her as the helicopter hovered level, Sarah brought the gun around and fired into the back of the pilot's head to ensure he was dead. Blood sprayed across the inside of the windshield.

Then Vivian left her.

As fast as she was there, she disappeared. The effort expended had been too great. Sarah felt that. Vivian felt that. There was no way to maintain that kind of connection for too long.

The exhaustion from the brief encounter made her want to sleep for days. The pain in her ribs had intensified in the minute she had been on the outside, clinging one-handed to the safety strap.

"You bitch," Enzo yelled as he clambered to his feet, a hand still clinging to his crotch. "You broke my nose."

She looked up at him from the floor of the chopper. "You're such an asshole."

She spun the gun around in her hand and swung, butt end first, at Enzo's left kneecap. She hit the top of his knee hard, the gun rattling in her hand. Enzo dropped like a broken elevator, writhing in pain, hitting the floor beside her.

She crawled onto him in her weakened state and pistol-whipped him in the nose, making more blood shoot out. He hollered in agony. She hit him repeatedly until his face was a ruined mush of flesh, bone, and broken teeth. He tried to resist and push her off, but the pain in his crotch, knee, and face weakened him. He could barely turn his face away to choke out the broken teeth bits.

The helicopter veered left. Then right. No one was at the controls. She had never flown one before and had no idea how.

She climbed off Enzo and struggled to the back of the front seats. The stick between the pilot's legs had to be what steered it.

One glance over her shoulder told her all she needed to know about Enzo. He was out cold as blood seeped along the floor toward the open door.

She hopped in the seat Enzo had occupied and pushed the stick gently to the left. The helicopter turned toward the house. Then she pushed the stick forward and quickly learned it changed the pitch of the main rotors. There were two foot pedals. She touched the one on the left, and the machine turned left. Then she tested the right, and it turned to the right.

How do I lower this thing?

On her left, beside the seat, sat a bar resembling a handbrake in a car. She touched it, hoping this was it, and gently pushed it down.

The helicopter responded instantly by dropping from its elevated position. Learning what did what in the chopper offered no illusion that she could successfully land it. But getting closer to the ground gave her a fighting chance when she jumped.

A hole formed in the bubble window to her left. Then another one formed as she steered the helicopter toward the grounds.

"They're shooting at me," she said to herself. "Enzo's men are shooting at me."

In the distance, on the house's roof, two black figures aimed at her and fired.

Bullets pinged off the helicopter. The windshield cracked and threatened to break altogether.

She jumped out of her seat and bumped the stick between her legs, knocking the chopper sideways. She lost her balance and fell into the dead pilot.

"Shit."

She twisted around, grabbed the stick, and righted the machine. It was back on course for the main house, a sprawling mansion with black figures on its roof firing madly at her.

She dropped in behind the pilot's seat and tried to think

of how to get out of there alive. When nothing came to her, she leaned over the seat and ensured the chopper was still aimed at the house. The helicopter, loaded with explosives, would smash into the house in thirty seconds, and Sarah had grown too weak to do anything about it.

She slumped behind the seat and stared out the window as the house drew closer.

I need to fly this thing somewhere else.

But she was too tired to get up. She slumped down farther. Then she prayed.

Vivian shouted in her head.

Sarah was too weak to listen.

Vivian shouted again, this time louder. Loud enough to make Sarah cover her ears.

Enzo was waking up. He held a knife in front of his bloody grotesque face. He advanced on her.

Jump ... Vivian shouted one more time.

But wasn't she out of time?

Enzo dove for her, the knife set to stab between the bones of her ribcage. Sarah pulled from a reserve of energy and rolled to avoid him, absolutely exhausted from the fight.

The ground was close. No one steered the chopper. It wobbled in the air, canted to the right, left, and back again.

Enzo held onto a safety strap and readied himself to jump on her again.

She rolled to get away from him, saw the helicopter dropping fast, and still headed directly for the house. They were going to crash in seconds.

Her consciousness waned as she rolled away from him one more time.

Enzo screamed in terror.

Sarah heard it from a distance as her eyes closed.

Chapter 46

AARON PEEKED AROUND THE thick tree he had been hiding behind. The men on the roof had turned to shoot at the approaching helicopter. Only one man remained, firing recklessly at the trees.

Malaka, the best shot among them, took careful aim, then squeezed the trigger. He missed.

After the required slew of curse words, he aimed and fired again. This time the man's head jerked back, and he disappeared from sight.

The rest of the gunfire was aimed at the chopper slowly approaching the house.

Darwin stepped from behind the guard shack. Parkman joined Aaron and stood at his side as Daniel, Alex, Bush, and the rest of Darwin's men crowded around them.

"Didn't Sarah get on that chopper?" Bush asked.

Darwin nodded. "She did."

"What the fuck do you think is going on?" Malaka asked.

"No idea," Darwin said, as if in a trance.

Through the light rain, Aaron saw the cockpit of the helicopter. One man lay slumped to the side. A blur of movement went on behind the pilot's seat. No one seemed to be flying the chopper.

A sickening feeling that—yet again—he would have to say goodbye to Sarah covered his body in sweat. He began chanting the word *no* as the chopper approached the main house.

Parkman started across the lawn. Daniel followed him. After a moment, Bush and Malaka ran ahead to offer cover fire if needed.

The helicopter disappeared from view for a brief moment as it swooped in low behind the house.

Time stood still. He couldn't hear anything, feel anything or do anything. His body numbed. Darwin shouted something beside him.

A loud crunch of metal shot across the open lawn as the helicopter crashed into the back of the huge mansion of the Enzo Cartel.

Aaron dropped to his knees, horrified at what his consciousness was digesting.

The house exploded in a fireball, knocking him backward at least five feet. Darwin landed two feet past him.

He looked up as chunks of wood, paneling, and glass rained around them. He couldn't see Parkman, Daniel, or Darwin's men. For a brief moment, they were obscured in the smoke.

Parkman, supported by Malaka, emerged from the smoke. Then Daniel, held by Bush. The foursome hobbled toward Aaron. They were mostly covered in black and red, bleeding from several spots. Aaron quickly assessed the wounds as not too serious. No puncture wounds. No missing eyeballs.

Aaron watched the fire rise from the center of what was once the house he saw as a prisoner in this compound. Breathing grew ragged as an acrid smell filled the air.

Sarah had been on that chopper. If she had jumped, she would die in the fall. If she had stayed inside the chopper, she was certainly dead.

He had to face the truth and come to terms with a new reality. Sarah couldn't have saved herself from this one. As much as he hoped she was still alive, he couldn't devise a reasonable play that allowed that possibility.

Sarah Roberts was finally dead.

Aaron gasped as he fainted.

Chapter 47

IT WAS ODD FOR her to hear the explosion and not be able to breathe. A slick cold enveloped her body, and her mind processed the feeling as death, a leaving of the body.

Like a life review before entering the gates of Heaven, thoughts of Aaron, her parents, and Parkman shot through her mind. What would they think? How would they feel about her posthumously? Was this Vivian's design from the beginning? Could she have done something different to save the people she loved from such grief? A vision of the Danube River in Europe entered her mind. All those years ago, fighting alongside Parkman in Hungary by a basilica in Esztergom. She had ended up in the river, almost died, then got on a helicopter and flown to safety. This time she was on a helicopter first. Then a river.

She still couldn't breathe but had to assume breathing wasn't something they did in Heaven.

Unless she wasn't in Heaven.

A river?

Blind panic rushed through her system. She opened her eyes and thrashed about. Dark, murky water surrounded her. An orange and gray sky floated above the surface of the water. Her ribs ached fiercely with the rhythmic pulsing of her lungs as they starved for air. She pushed upward and broke the water's surface, where she gasped oxygen in like candy after a year's anti-sugar diet.

Everything ached as she turned to float on her back and breathe. Breathing was good. For now, that's all she wanted. Fresh air.

The house burned a hundred yards away. She watched it, knowing Enzo was dead. The men who had been shooting from the roof were dead.

She was prepared to do what Aaron and Casper had done and walk away from this place. But first, a rest. Weariness had settled in after all the energy she used fighting Enzo, and she hadn't eaten anything in ages.

After a few minutes, she swam lightly to the edge and discovered she was in a reservoir. She climbed over the rim, needing to leave before fire trucks and police arrived. Being found here would make for too many questions.

She rolled off the side and landed gently on a platform. The platform shielded her from the house where the flames had lost most of their orange color, turning yellow with black smoke billowing into the gray sky.

She closed her eyes and laid her head down softly. Maybe a five-minute rest first. Then she could be on her way. Standing and walking out of there seemed impossible on the little strength she had left.

A little rest, then walk.
Just a little …

Chapter 48

AARON WOKE TO THE sensation of being carried.

"Put me down," he said.

Malaka set him on his feet. "You fainted. Boss wants us out of here before the authorities show up."

Aaron nodded once and turned back to the house. It was almost all smoke now, with yellow flames emanating from the center.

"Oh, Sarah …"

"Aaron," Parkman said. "I'm so sorry." Parkman was crying. He wrapped his arms around Aaron. "If there were anything I could do, I'd do it. Just let me take her place." His voice cracked, and he stopped talking.

"Me too, Parkman. Me too, man." They held each other and wept.

"Guys," Darwin whispered. "I'm pissed now. I'll grieve later. You grieve later, too. No choice. We need to move out now. Can't be found when the authorities get here. Cool?"

Aaron felt Parkman nod against his shoulder, then they parted. Casper came up beside Aaron and wrapped an arm around his shoulder.

"I only knew her for a short time," Casper said. "But it was enough to know she was one hell of a woman."

Aaron nodded, not trusting his voice to say anything.

"All I could picture was you and me in that helicopter. Those guys Alejandro tossed out." Casper shook his head and stared at the ground as they walked. "Sarah knew you'd die for her. I saw you jump myself—"

Aaron stopped walking and went rigid. Casper's arm slipped off his shoulder.

"What?" Casper asked. "Was it something I said?"

"The reservoir."

Casper snapped his fingers. "That's right. It's a chance. But what if she didn't see it?"

"She didn't need to see it."

Aaron turned and ran toward the stables.

"What do you mean?" Casper yelled after him.

"Only Vivian needed to see it." Aaron spun around and ran backward for a moment. "Get the RV. Drive around to the back and pick me up."

Sirens roared in the distance.

Casper, Parkman, Darwin, and his men ran for the RV as Aaron bolted for the reservoir.

He made it there in five minutes flat. The sirens were coming up the road at the front of the house, but he was shielded from the fire until he reached the other side of the reservoir.

There was no kidding himself. This was probably a dead-end. But even if there was a smidgen of hope, he had to look.

He climbed a small ladder that led to a metal walkway that bordered the reservoir on all four sides. As fast as he could run, he headed down the length of one side, turned left to run the next walkway, and stopped dead in his tracks.

Sarah Roberts lay sleeping on the walkway up ahead. His Sarah. *The* Sarah. Alive. Before approaching her, he wiped the water from his eyes to see her better.

"Sarah ..." his voice broke.

He dropped beside her and checked for a pulse. Weak, but there. Instead of waking her, he lifted her into a sitting position, placed his shoulder in her stomach, and brought her up until she draped over his shoulder, his right arm holding her close by the backs of her knees.

Then Aaron carried her off the walkway, down the steps, and across the grass, until he reached the road in the back, his mind numb the whole way. How many lives did Sarah have? He would make her promise to go on a vacation. This one had been too close. But what a relief to find her alive.

And they almost left her there. What kind of a man leaves his woman behind? From now on, he committed to exhaust all avenues and leave nothing to chance regarding Sarah. If he didn't find her body or bones, she would be considered alive. That's how it had to be when dealing with Sarah because she was too hard to kill.

The RV pulled up. Parkman jumped out before Daniel fully stopped the vehicle.

They helped Sarah inside and placed her on the back bed where Benjamin still slept.

Daniel turned the RV around, drove away from the ruined Enzo Cartel compound, and headed for the border.

Aaron collapsed at the edge of the bed, holding Sarah's hand, and forgot everyone else for a time as he wept, her hand pressed gently into his cheek.

Chapter 49

THE VEHICLE CAME TO a stop, the engine revs lowering. She opened her eyes, disorientation waxing over her.

Vehicle?

A camper on wheels. She lay on the bed, Aaron holding her hand. He was staring at her inner elbow, where Eduardo shot her up with heroin several times.

Aaron's bloodshot eyes turned toward her. They locked eyes briefly, then he leaned in and gently hugged her.

"I thought you were gone for good. I'm so glad you're still with us."

"Where would I have gone?" she asked. "How did you find me?"

Aaron lifted his head. "I knew about the reservoir. Figured you'd use it."

The RV edged forward, then stopped.

"Name everyone."

"What?"

"Tell me who is in this camper thing with us."

Aaron told her all the names, even Darwin's mercenaries. Casper came back to tell her she was one tough woman. Parkman made an appearance and hugged her gently.

"I don't want to get up just yet. Ribs ache."

Parkman nodded and left her with Aaron.

"We have so much to talk about," Aaron said.

"Yes, we do. Let me see your finger."

Aaron raised the bandaged appendage. "Once we're home, I'll get this properly cleaned. It'll be okay. I can still work with it gone."

"I'm sorry they did this to you," Sarah said.

"I know, baby." He looked at her arm. "I'm sorry they did that to you."

She was already feeling the urge. One little fix, and she'd be all set. She wouldn't touch the stuff ever again. Just one more fix.

"It's fine," she said. "I'll get over it."

His face softened, and he offered her a half smile. "Any chance you could take a break? A vacation? I felt like I lost you back there."

"I was thinking the same thing. This is it for a while. I need to heal, work out, and eat a full meal. I'm starving."

"Are you going to have issues with that?" he asked, gesturing at her inner elbow. "Those tracks tell a story."

She looked at her arm, then averted her eyes. "No. But if I do, I will get treatment and rehab. It's not an issue because it wasn't my fault. I couldn't stop them. I'll beat it. I'm stronger than any substance."

She hoped her eyes didn't betray her as she had just

betrayed Aaron. If heroin were beside her, she wouldn't ignore it. She would shoot up. At least once more. But she couldn't tell anyone that because she would beat it and never feel the urge again. She decided to blame her weakened state for the urge. It had to be that. Nothing else. Thinking about it, and having Aaron bring it up, only made her yearn for one more fix. Just one, then it would be truly over.

"I didn't mean anything by it," he said.

She closed her eyes as the RV moved again. "Where are we?"

"At the Mexican border. We're about to enter the States."

She opened her eyes and stared up at the ceiling. "With mercenaries on board? Isn't that risky?"

"Casper made a call. They're expecting us. Some kind of diplomatic immunity for this vehicle."

She smiled. "I'm sure glad that guy's still alive. He's good for something, eh?"

Aaron nodded beside her. "He sure is. Probably wouldn't have escaped the compound if it wasn't for him."

"I'm so glad everyone is here. I can't believe the friends I have."

Benjamin woke beside her and tried to sit up. "Yeah, I can't believe the friends I have. Took a bullet for them."

They laughed together. Sarah's urge increased. She needed a fix, or she was going to withdraw. She wasn't sure what withdrawal symptoms were like as she'd never had heroin before. Would the withdrawal be that bad? She'd only been high for a few days. But it was a permanent high. They'd kept shooting shit into her veins. The unknown weakened her resolve. She detested weakness and had never felt so weak in her life.

I'll beat this, right, sis?

"One thing is for sure," Aaron said. "We need a vacation."

"Take me to my parents in Santa Rosa. Give me a day or two, and then we will find a beach hotel somewhere and turn the world off for a few weeks. Deal?"

"Turn off the world, this one and the one on the other side?"

"Yes, Vivian too."

"Deal." Aaron turned to the rest of the men in the RV. "Guys, we're officially on vacation."

A small congratulations and cheers went up, then died. Daniel pulled closer to the border. Sarah squirmed on the bed. Her forehead beaded up in a sweat. This wasn't like her. Feelings of need and weakness didn't become her. She left a part of herself back at the compound. She lost something back there, and it would take considerable effort and time to get it back. If she didn't get a small fix, Aaron would think he was losing her, and she never wanted him to ever feel that he was losing her.

A small fix ... or Losing Sarah.

"Yeah, a bloody vacation," she whispered. "Brilliant."

The RV edged closer to the border.

Afterword

DEAR READER,

I wanted to address cartels in this novel due to the seriousness of their existence. The amount of cocaine entering through America's southern border is incredible. Canada too. Cartels are responsible for ninety percent of the cocaine entering the U.S. alone. Cartels have wholesale earnings estimated as high as fifty billion per year. When they arrest the leader of a cartel, violence escalates as rival cartels move in to fill the void and claim the disputed territory as their own.

Currently, the Sinaloa Cartel and the Gulf Cartel have taken the trafficking of cocaine from Columbia to worldwide markets.

But they're a relatively new thing. The birth of the Mexican cartel is traced back to 1980 when Miguel Gallardo

—"The Godfather"—founded the Guadalajara Cartel. He was a former Mexican Judicial Federal Police agent.

Among the atrocities attributed to cartels in 2011, 177 bodies were discovered in a mass grave in Tamaulipas. It's the same area where seventy-two migrants' bodies were found in 2010.

Just recently, on September 26, 2014, forty-three students on a trip went missing. Mexican authorities suggest local law enforcement took part in a shootout that night where buses carrying dozens of students and soccer players were attacked. When the authorities came to this southern Mexican town to search for the missing students, they found unmarked mass graves of other victims. Twenty-eight bodies were covered in gasoline and burned before they were buried. Too brutal for reality.

You have probably heard that El Chapo, the Sinaloa Cartel drug lord, recently escaped. And the saga continues.

In April 2015, CNN announced that DEA agents have been attending sex parties filled with prostitutes, paid for by drug cartels. They discovered that drug cartels have organized fifteen to twenty parties. In some cases, DEA agents have received expensive gifts and weapons from cartels. One DEA agent beat a prostitute over a payment dispute and received a two-week unpaid leave as punishment. His security clearance wasn't revoked. He wasn't fired. He wasn't disciplined further. In fact, no DEA agent has been fired for their actions in partaking in these cartel-bought and paid-for hooker parties.

I chose Tijuana for this novel because it's a major portal city to the north. There were 844 homicides in Tijuana in 2008, more than double Detroit. Cartels are always looking for more dreadful ways to kill and stimulate fear in their enemies.

Hugo Hernandez, twenty-six years old, was kidnapped from Sonora in 2010. A week later, they found his corpse in the city of Los Mochis. He'd been chopped to pieces. His face had been skinned off and stitched to a soccer ball.

Finally, and not to belabor the point, let me add more.

Masked gunmen dump thirty-five bodies on the street during rush hour in Mexico. Twitter lit up immediately as drivers tried to warn others to avoid the area.

A female blogger who routinely blogged about drug traffickers was found decapitated, her head atop the keyboard she typed her blogs on.

There are hundreds of other stories, hence the reason I wanted Sarah to fight a cartel.

Here's the good part—names in this novel were used as an ongoing program I'm doing with readers. If you ever want your name featured in a book, email me at jonassaul@icloud.com. Or if you just want to say hello or state an opinion, hit me up.

Credit and thanks go to:

Ellen Burns - Parkman's safe house special agent #1.

Kira Junod - Parkman's safe house special agent #2.

Tessa McCurry - Sarah's sassy nurse in the Mexican hospital when she cracked a rib.

Book group/writer group members of WASP—Writers, Artists, Specialists, and Perusers. Here they are:

Alexia Purdy - President

Sandra Gonzales - Vice President

Debbie Lyons - alter ego Penelope

Charlotte Cross - Researcher

Lesley Weiler

Lavern Skipper

Debra Smith

Lisa Wesley

Thank you to everyone who allowed me to use your names and for saving Sarah's life. If WASP didn't show up at the compound when they did, Sarah might've died in the barn. Because they were at the gate, they delayed Enzo so long that he took her on the helicopter in his feeble attempt to escape his own compound. So thanks for that.

And thanks for reading. Not just the people above but all of you. Thanks for coming back, time and again, to see what Sarah is up to. I love you all and wish you the best wherever you are. And know you're in my thoughts as I'm eternally grateful to have you as readers. I couldn't do this without you. No, really, I couldn't.

Great pains are taken to ensure everything in this novel is accurate and error-free. Any and all mistakes that might appear are mine and mine alone.

Stay safe, be well, and take care of yourself and each other. And get caught reading …

Love,

Jonas

About Jonas Saul

Jonas Saul is the bestselling author of the Sarah Roberts Series—more than two million sold!—and has written and published over sixty thrillers. After acquiring an agent, he signed several deals in Los Angeles, with MadRiver Pictures optioning his Sarah Roberts Series— over forty books!—(currently in development).

Jonas has often outranked Stephen King and Dean

Koontz on Amazon over the past decade. He's regularly invited to be a guest speaker, teacher, or workshop presenter at international writing conferences and film festivals worldwide. He hosts an annual writer's retreat in Greece, where he currently lives. He focuses his teaching on how to get tension and emotion in every scene, on every page, how he made it as a creator/writer, the path to success in this business, and the pitfalls to avoid. He also hosts a reading retreat in Greece with guest authors, yoga retreats, and hiking retreats. Visit the Imagine Greece Retreats website at www.imaginegreeceretreats.com, or email him directly to discuss an opportunity to join one of the retreats at jonas@imaginegreeceretreats.com.

Jonas is also a professional freelance editor. He works for several publishers and does private editing for clients, with many testimonials on his website at www.imaginepress.org, which details each author's response to Jonas's editing skills. Email Jonas directly for an editing quote at editor@imaginepress.org.

To book Jonas for a speaking engagement at a writer's conference/festival, to have him on your jury at a film festival, or even to say hello, email Jonas directly at jonassaul@icloud.com.

For updates on releases, hit the "Follow" button on Amazon or Bookbub, and join Jonas on Facebook, where he's most active.

Contact Jonas Saul

Linktree: Find me here

Email: jonassaul@icloud.com